Yesterday Is Today

N. O.

Copyright © 2015 N. O.
All rights reserved.

ISBN: 151162972X
ISBN 13: 9781511629720

SPECIAL ACKNOWLEDGMENT

Special thanks to my editor **Ombonia Waits** (who also edited Silent Cry) for his diligence and for having a keen eye for detail in making this book possible.

Thanks to Mr. John Carrington and Heaven 600 Radio for allowing me the opportunity of a guest appearance to speak about my book.

My appreciation to everyone who supported me, and read my first book **Silent Cry**, I hope that you enjoy this novel as well.

TABLE OF CONTENTS

Change Of Pace	1
F.Y.I	4
Hard To Get	6
Fear Not	10
Beware	15
Playboy on the Prowl	21
I.M.O.L (Indecent Moment Of Lust)	26
Inquiring Minds	36
New Acquaintance	42
Kill Joy	44
I Remember When	47
Birds of A Feather	51
Mind Games	59
Fair For the Goose	67
Sweet and Sour	73
Prisoner of A Nymph	80
Ace in the Hole	93
One Too Many	97
Yesterday Is Gone	103
Release Me	109
This Is It	117

CHANGE OF PACE

Rachelle WynHurst sat quietly in her living room. She gazed out of the window to a gloomy winter morning. This time the meteorologist weather prediction was correct. In the state of Delaware, snow accumulation was six to eight inches, maybe more. Those conditions always saddened and depressed her mood. Cheery was not the word of the day for her.

Her present state of mind was in a whirlwind. In her wonderment many questions required answers, but where to start was not in the cards. Rachelle's current life was a bit unstable. *Why?* Her inner self wanted to know. *How did I get to this point?* That particular one bothered her as much. *Where did I go wrong?* That puzzled her also.

Rachelle saw herself as a loving and caring individual; she had so much to give. Yet life's unpleasant face always, somehow, managed to disrupt her every intention. So Rachelle lingered here—single again, lonely—in a maze of uncertainty, concerning the future.

The only joy she had now was her two grown children. Anthony Jr. was 22. His sister, Antionette was 20. They were the apple of her eye. The latter was still in college, studying to become a doctor of pediatrics; and the former was a practicing attorney.

Anthony, their father, disappeared shortly after Antionette's birth. Rachelle saw the deadbeat dad as an asshole and lowdown dirty scum for abandoning his children. In spite of that, the thought of him, at times, brought overwhelming chills to her. Her passion for the man would somehow strangely resurface. During such spells, uncontrollable memories would set in and remind Rachelle of the past and how she first met Anthony.

◈

She quickly reminded herself to think of pleasant thoughts, such as Lori and Lisa, close friends, who had convinced Rachelle to go out for dinner at Deuce's.

The popular club was well known for its mouth-watering menu selections (food and drink), and smooth easy-listening jazz.

N. O.

This night her girls ordered their usual, apple martini, while Rachelle preferred a milder mixed drink, fuzzy navel. The three had been buddies for more than twenty years. Their girlie conversations usually covered a variety of topics; but for some reason it always started and ended with sex.

At this time, Rachelle really welcomed her good friends company. She needed a change of pace because all work and no play made for a dull and boring woman. Anyway these days, Rachelle was getting her life in order, and the present company helped with the situation.

These ladies were so busy and deep into Lori's graphic, sexual activity details that none had noticed or heard the request of the stranger who approached their table. Nevertheless, he stood there patiently as the gossipy women carried on and on; and it was mostly about the biological make-up of the male physique. The curiosity was rather interesting.

Finally, Rachelle noticed their uninvited guest—after he had gotten an earful of the apparent warmed-up mess. However, her spirited attempt at quieting Lori was all in vain. The very talkative friend was on a roll and there simply was no stopping her. Rachelle gave "miss mouthy" a swift kick on the leg. And that obviously necessary action caused Lori to jump suddenly and through clenched teeth she squealed, "shit!"

The handsome intruder was so manly amused, and with a faint grin, he introduced himself by first clearing his throat as a gentleman might.

"Hi there, I'm Kirk..." His initial effort was not successful. He only wanted to join the seemingly fun girls because seating was limited after 9pm. "Hey ladies," they heard him the second time, "mind if I have a seat?"

Kirk had nice manners up front. The girlfriends nodded in agreement. *Okay.* They each had drawn an opinion that the very sharp dressed guy meant well.

So then what harm would come to them from sharing a table with a good-looking stranger? *Probably none.* Besides, there was one of him—and three of them. The friends looked at each other, uncertain as to who between them would speak for the trio. Lori took the duty upon herself.

"Sit here," she gestured toward the vacant space between her and Lisa.

"That'll work," Kirk smiled as he excused himself and took a seat. "Are you ladies enjoying yourselves?"

"So far so good," Lori responded. Her tone was a pleasant opening.

"I'm having a great time." Lisa was jovial. "The food is tasty and the drink master really knows his stuff."

"How about you" he asked looking at Rachelle.

"It's too early to tell," she replied, "however, I really liked the lump crab cake dinner."

Then Rachelle focused her divided attention towards the band and briefly studied the attire of the men and women in the very spacious club. Some of the women wore their Sunday best, while others actually missed the fine garment mark. The men were simply dressed to impress. Everybody seemed content with the inside atmosphere.

Deuce's could draw a pretty good crowd on nights such as this one. The cozy club was located in a very nice section of town; where many independent stores, shops, restaurants, clubs, and other businesses flourished. So, folks were naturally drawn to this "nice time" oasis.

F.Y.I.

Lori, the go getter, dived right in with her interrogation of Kirk. "Are you married?" She squinted. "Do you have children?" Her chin was in hand. He was not allowed room for thought. "What type of work you do?" Lori was determined, with no plans to reduce the rudeness.

Anything and everything her mind could think of was pitched in Kirk's direction until Lisa finally came to the rescue, changing the subject. She and Rachelle found humor, as Kirk wondered whether Lori was a private eye, law enforcement, or just plain nosey.

Lisa was more interested in the man's physical make-up. She tried not to appear so obvious. She measured him to be about six feet, seven inches, maybe one hundred and ninety pounds. Kirk had a nice butt, great biceps, and full front package. His was of malt chocolate complexion; a shaved head with no facial hair, except a well trimmed mustache—above a pair inviting lips. Lisa was sure.

Kirk's attire was impressive. *I could sure give him the time of his life.* Lisa thought. But that would not be so easy; Lori was hot and heavy all over him. Rachelle's direct attention was to the band. Smooth Jazz always took her to another dimension; she felt romantic, calm and relaxed. Yet her ears were open to the double-dutch conversation of her table-mates.

The band played one of Rachelle's favorites, "Some Enchanted Evening", before taking their first break. As the musicians left the stage, she noticed the saxophone player smiling; he headed toward her. He stopped where she was seated, asking her name without giving his.

That approach really pissed her off. Rachelle thought he was rude. He gave, and she felt, the impression that he was God's gift to women. Although she sensed that his looks could warm a cold body on any day, she simply looked away. No way, she was going to be taken by a handsome face. Looks were just that...looks. What else did he have to offer?

Ignoring him, a nonchalant Rachelle sipped her drink and continued to block out *Mr. Good Looks* and his surly attitude. This was a signal to back-off, that she was not interested. Rachelle could guess that he wanted more than she was willing to give.

Lisa and Lori continued to wear Kirk down with the back and forth to win his attention. The poor guy was drinking like a fish, to evade the battle commanders. Ordinarily, Kirk could handle alcohol. He usually had a couple drinks. To ignore them, he did everything he could to talk with Rachelle, but she was pre-occupied.

But Kirk was turned on by her manner. The way she tilted her head, was apparently in deep thought; and how her lips pressed against the glass when taking a sip. Her stature glowed like polished gold. That was not to mention, Rachelle's smile warmed him as no other.

This attractive babe's stylish appearance was lady-like. A powder blue dress stopped about six inches above her knee; it complemented her complexion and figure. Rachelle's reddish brown and shoulder length hair was her own—no weave or extensions. It flowed freely with each graceful movement. One could say that she had lots of class and carried it very well.

HARD TO GET

Rachelle sensed that Kirk had eyes for her. She was out for a night with her friends and musical entertainment; not male interaction. She calmly sipped her drink, looked around and observed others in the club. Funny how some things never change. To her it was obvious who were sincerely into whom, as opposed to others standing out like a sore thumb—for a one night stand.

On his way back from intermission, the saxophonist stopped at Rachelle's table once again. This time he appeared more civil. He introduced himself as Cedric and apologized for his behavior. With anticipation he waited for her to acknowledge his plea.

Rachelle's intension was not to rush accepting anything from Cedric. Her penetrating stare was a bit un-nerving; as though a thousand needles pierced his body. This was a soul searching moment, seemingly extended in time.

"I can't say that I am pleased to meet you," she was not pleasant. She paused.

"I'm Rachelle, and I accept your apology," she finally replied in a rather cold tone.

She slowly looked away, to converse with the threesome, Lori, Lisa, and Kirk. They were at a loss for verbal communication. Body language was a tip of their silence. Each expression was a direct message to the other. Rachelle obliged to Cedric, clearly received. His appeal was not truly sincere to her. Something about his eyes warned her that he was not to be trusted.

Cedric was caught off guard. He was not accustomed to any female responding in that manner. After all, he had gone out of his way apologizing. Trying to smooth out the roughness of the first time was not part of his M.O. (mode of operation).

Cedric excused himself sheepishly, returning to play. And that they did well. Their melodic mind-soothing mixes caused ooh and ahs all over. Then, it never hurts to throw in an oldie-but-goodie here and there. They did favorites such as *Mass Confusion* for jazz heads;

Misty, Bridge over Troubled Water, for R&B lovers, and many other tunes reminding them of yesterday. Good music fed their hearts.

Kirk felt good witnessing the slam dunk Rachelle delivered swiftly to Cedric. That was an opening to finally muster courage to ask her to dance.

"Well, that was a first," Kirk extended a hand. "Lady, may I have the honor?"

Rachelle generally did not care for slow jams with strangers. But, she felt it would be OK to make an exception for Kirk; after all, he appeared to be a really nice, respectful guy.

"I guess so, but only if you explain the remark you just made," Rachelle smiled at him. She waited unremittingly for a response.

"If you insist," he prolonged the answer.

"I do," Rachelle smirked. "Now stop dodging the issue. Answer the question or no dance." She was dead serious.

Kirk did not want her ego tripping by what he was about to admit.

"OK," he was reluctant. "You're the only female I know whoever talked like that to Cedric. " He took another drink. "He didn't have a *come-back-at-you* remark for you lady."

Kirk knew that Cedric could be rough and tough with mouthy women. That was him. The guy put the "S" in shrewd.

"Now, there you have it," he was concerned. "But, be careful, stay on your toes."

Kirk grabbed Rachelle's hand quickly, intending to escort her to the floor briskly. It did not happen. She anticipated his move, taking her time promenading towards the dance area.

Kirk held her a little too close. Rachelle put distance between the two bodies skillfully. They glided together somewhat appropriately as strangers. He was a good dancer, considerate of her in-affectionate embrace.

Cedric, the pissed-off saxophone player, could not keep his eyes off them. Rachelle's effort to avoid attention did not help. She glanced briefly in his direction, feeling a warm sensation by his intense stare. He wanted her to notice, but she would do that when ready, not before.

Rachelle was determined to keep an upper hand, calling his bluff. Kirk's warning that Cedric was use to playing women rang clearly in her ear. Little did Cedric know; tonight would be the beginning of something he, so called master, would have no control over.

She was surely impressed with his looks. The guy was really put together nicely. Cedric had a youthful appearance. Rachelle guessed his age maybe about forty-five. His body from what she had observed; was that of someone who might frequent the gym three to five days a week.

Kirk gave up any hope of getting next to Rachelle before their dance ended. He was no dummy, knowing he was out of his league. Besides, the friction ignited between Cedric and she was too hyped for him. He quickly added one plus one as two. Kirk understood the threatening looks sent his way.

"Damn musicians think they rule the world," he was really angered, "who the hell do he think he is that every woman should bow at his feet?"

Kirk knew that two could play Cedric's game, sending warning stares. He had a few of his own and directed them in the player's direction. He put his face closer to the right side of Rachelle's head and imagined that they were someplace other than where they were.

His move surely caused Cedric's blood to boil. Kirk wanted him to know that this brother was not moving aside, because of the *big slick wolf*. Free will meant just that. Kirk Bevins was stepping away for his own good reason—by choice.

He was well aware that Cedric could be dangerous with someone or something in his way. His reputation, no doubt preceded him. No right mind dared to step on his toes.

Kirk had heard that Cedric was much older than he looked. One of his ex-girl friends' had seen his driver's license that confirmed him to be late sixties, early seventies. Then he had briefly seen the senior citizen in action. And the man had handled himself better than Kirk, who was early forties. Some had mistakenly taken Cedric's young looks, as being someone they could walk over, but quickly found that not to be true.

"Why am I tripping," he asked himself.

There was always more than one fish in the sea. It was clear, Lori liked Kirk. He would direct his sights to her. *Why not?* She was a nice person, and intelligent he gathered from their conversation thus far. Although Lori was a little too inquisitive, he could live with that. Hell, he had spent most of the night listening to her rattle on, almost non-stop. That point was not to mention, that chick's body was a knock-out.

He walked Rachelle back to her seat politely, and gestured immediately to Lori.

"Come on baby, it's you and me," grinning as he pulled her from the seat to dance.

FEAR NOT

Kirk's numerous drinks gave him more courage than ever imagined. That's right. He was the only guy in the club, in the company of three gorgeous women. The *eyeball-bully* band member could stare all night; but Kirk was not about to tuck his tail and run cowardly.

The women were enjoying him and vice-visa. Not only did Kirk have Lori and Lisa's attention, but Rachelle's as well. The foolish sax player could blow himself and his horn full of air, until collapsing. In spite of that, Kirk was having the time of his life.

Cedric's reputation did not matter to him. He wasn't afraid of the guy, just wanted to stay clear of him. Kirk did not have to walk into fire to get burnt. If Cedric wanted to start trouble because the woman he desired would not give him the time of day, then so be it. And bring it on!

If anything, Cedric had better know that Mr. Kirk Bevins could hold his own; if and wherever necessary. The grapevine had it that Cedric nearly beat a guy to death, just for looking at one of his ladies. Another word: a guy lost his grill (teeth) by a first-hand introduction to Cedric's hard left hook. He had commented how hot the chick looked in a mini-skirt.

Kirk was on a roll, laughing and drinking with Rachelle and her friends, but he still thought Cedric was capable of—quickly taking a brother out.

Most of his buddies knew that Cedric put a *hit* on a guy who took one of his women. Kirk did not get the full story, but the man was never seen again.

"I'm not leaving town or disappearing, and that's for sure," he mumbled.

Rachelle did not appear worried, so why would he?
Serves him right, meeting his match, Kirk thought.

Little was known about Cedric's family, except that he had a son. It was said that they could pass for identical twins. Kirk had to admit that Cedric did look great for his assumed age.

Hell, damn man looks younger than me! Kirk thought.

The hair on the back of Kirk's neck was aflame; his attempt to ignore Cedric did not shake the feeling—something bad was about to happen.

Nightly entertainment was about to end. But now everything was cool. Kirk did not think Cedric would start anything with Rachelle and friends watching. He needed to play his cards right—not to get decked by a thug.

So he decided to ride it out, drinking, dancing, and enjoying himself. The music soothed with Lori's body close to his. She too noticed Cedric's mean looks toward Kirk, but remained silent. Her sharp curiosity required so much, yet she did not want to obstruct the mood of the moment. Lori had finally met someone to connect with. The saxophone player was not a priority.

Kirk is so cool. I really like him, and surely hope the feeling is mutual. Lori thought.

She could see this acquaintance going to another level. Lori was not intimidated by the way Kirk flirted with Rachelle in the beginning. He had weighed his options then. Kirk only did what any guy in the company of three sexy women would do.

Sometime men underestimate loyalty of some women. Rachelle, Lisa, and she, never back stabbed when it came to the other's mate. They had respect for themselves, and one another.

Lori would have backed off if Kirk wanted to hook-up with either of them. Her buddies knew she wanted Kirk for herself. Lisa focused her attention on a guy who appeared fascinated, with the way she handled herself on the dance floor. Afterwards, they struck up a conversation that blocked out all, but them.

Rachelle was in her own world, and although the *music man* was hot on her heels, she had brushed him off. Lori was amused, because she knew that if he really wanted her friend he would need to do better, than what she had witnessed. Rachelle's life was complicated and there was no room for BS (bull-shit).

Lori had Kirk all to herself; now was the opportunity to see what made this man tick. She was not about to waste time with a good looking loser. Kirk did not project this, but she was not taking any chances.

Even though there was her non-stop questioning towards Kirk earlier, Lori kept a watchful-eye and alert ear. So far Kirk had passed. He seemed to have morals, respected women, and was truly funny. Lori liked being in his company.

Yet, there were more questions that needed answers; such as what was with him and Cedric. She knew nothing about the band player, but something about his demeanor made her a bit uncomfortable. Lori intended to keep a keen eye on him.

"Are you OK," Kirk asked.

He sensed something was consuming Lori's attention. She had lost step, hand dancing, and for some reason she was watching Cedric, as if he was the *big bad wolf.*

"I'm fine," Lori smiled, "sorry I got a little clumsy. I know it's not a good feeling when someone attacks your toes dancing." She lowered her head teasing.

"My toes are fine," Kirk responded, "it's my spit-shine that's ruined." He joked.

"Don't be funny, your foot ware is so bright, I need shades," she continued, "who massages your shoes? I need their number."

Humor was good, getting to know someone. Lori thought it was good that she and Kirk could joke and keep things going lightly.

It was clear that he cared about his appearance. That was surely a plus; Lori loved seeing a guy in a nice suit, dressed not only to impress, but to turn heads as well.

They headed back to their seats, holding hands like school kids. Someone Kirk knew stopped on his way to the bar.

"Hey man, what's going on? The fellows were wondering, who the lucky dude was with three of the prettiest women in the club. Well, get out the mirror, it's one of our own."

"What can I say? They like the way I handle myself," Kirk was smooth. "I have been trying to catch you. Still on the move, huh?"

"Are you going to introduce me or not," he asked.

"Don't be so anxious man," Kirk amused.

"Jeffrey, this is Lori, the investigator," Kirk began, "hands off if you know what I mean." He was serious.

"Rachelle, the quiet one," he went on, "so look-out." He winked.

"And Lisa, the observer," he stared at Jeffrey.

"Ladies, Jeff is a good friend of mine," Kirk concluded, "we go way back."

Now that the introductions were over, the stage was set. His job was done. The rest was on his buddy.

"Wow! I am really pleased to meet you ladies," Jeff was excited. "Take a walk with me man, need to bend your ear."

Cedric's buddy was easy on the eye. He was about six feet, two inches in height, maybe one hundred and eighty pounds. He had an impressive executive appearance; the suit was definitely tailor made.

"Be nice ladies," Kirk smiled, "I'll be right back." He pointed at them.

Then he ordered drinks, from the floor waitress, for Lori and her friends.

"I got this," Jeff insisted reaching in his pocket, "you know how we roll."

"OK bro, big time spender," Kirk gave his friend the knuckle salute.

They did roll like that, always having each other's back. They had been good guy friends since elementary school, many years ago. They then attended the same East Coast College; and they ironically majored in the same field…law. Jeffrey had a very successful private practice, specializing in criminal defense.

Kirk was a well respected prosecutor, known for his aggressive court room tactics. His conviction rate was well above average. He had won many high profile cases. One of them involved the murder of a mother and her three children, by a deranged landscaper. The four went missing for nearly two years. They were found buried in their pool area.

A neighbor questioned, reported to the police that she saw the hired worker dragging something that looked odd. She had stated that she could not understand his reason for working on the new pool that time of night. It was dark, no light.

The suspect was questioned, and once his alibi was cleared, released. But the witness who lived nearby really felt that it was he who had committed the crime. She was persistent with concern. But police continued to ignore her plea.

After all, she and the family were close. The mother of the three children was having an affair with the grounds-keeper. And her husband's job required late hours; and at times travel away from home. This did not leave much quality time for wife and kids.

Somehow he found out about the two lovers. The wife ended the affair, which was not taken well by the adultery partner.

BEWARE

"So how long have you known the three foxy ladies?" Jeff wanted to know. He was really intrigued by the women.

"I just met them tonight," Kirk answered, "they were here when I arrived." He felt that Jeffrey had more questions.

"You know how it is at Deuce's on the weekend after 9pm." He leaned against the bar, looking at the crowd.

"I couldn't find a seat, and *voila*, there they were."

Kirk's French was evidently limited; and Jeff thought it was funny.

"I asked if I could share their table," Kirk said, "and the rest is history." He hit Jeff on the shoulder.

"All I can say is that you are one lucky SOB," Jeff replied and returned a friendly punch.

"I know Lori is off-limits, you made that clear," he went on, "but what about Rachelle and Lisa?"

"I have no idea," Kirk was truthful. He sipped his drink. "My feeling is, go for it, but keep in mind, I'm not a psychic."

"Man, I needed to get you alone," Jeff was concerned. "I heard disturbing news of foul-play involving Cedric."

"Go on, don't have me dangling," Kirk frowned.

"I just want you to be careful," Jeff warned. He leaned closer so no one else could hear.

"We know our man on the horn is a bit shady," he continued. Kirk listened intently.

"Remember the dude who hit on his chick," he reminded carefully, "and afterwards disappeared?"

Jeff did not mind telling him all he knew about it. And it was a difficult task. Even he did not want to recall that bit of news.

"Well, they found a body fitting his description," he concluded, "down by the tracks yesterday." As Jeff finished, he looked rather weird.

"Man, I thought that guy skipped town," Kirk remarked quickly, "after Cedric busted him up pretty bad."

There was always more than one side to every story; and he had his own account of what really took place. Actually, nobody knew exactly what had happened.

"So, do they know who took him out," Kirk asked. He was so certain that Cedric had a hand in it.

"No, but to be honest," Jeff admitted, "the guys and myself were checking Cedric out."

Kirk felt that Cedric's reaching out—like strong claws—was ready to seize one of the women at the table—Rachelle in particular.

"Another buddy was uneasy," Jeff said, "about the way you and Cedric were going at it with all the stares."

Kirk knew all too well what he was saying. He stood speechless, but not in denial. Cedric, no doubt, had never been charged with any crimes. And those who could bear witness would never put their lives in jeopardy, anyway.

"Have you ever noticed, any woman his sights is on, is a no-no by Cedric's law?" Kirk said.

The ruthless womanizer was known for claim jumping, if it had to be told. And this guy felt obligated.

"But it's fine for him to tread your turf?" Kirk was pissed.

The informant looked disgusted. Perhaps he had distaste for lowlife. Men like Cedric cared nothing about the code among men. It was not very wise to backstab. He was known to take another man's woman, and think nothing of it. The guys all agreed that it seemed to turn him on; just getting away with it.

"Yeah man, I have," Jeff said, "and I say we should bum-rush his bad ass."

They were on the same page. Whipping his butt would have been very satisfying. They both laughed at the possibility of that thought becoming a reality.

Dangerous Cedric needed to be taken out of commission. But then, tonight was not the time. Kirk was really feeling the alcohol; but was not about to have his body wash-up on shore, tracks, or anywhere.

"All I'm saying is watch your back." Jeff only wanted him to be on guard.

It was no secret how shrewd Cedric could be. The man was cunning, cold-blooded and tricky. It really paid to stay on your toes; the way the old saying goes. Who was to say how many more bodies would surface. He really did not play by the book, and made his own rules. Cedric was big-time in his own way, not penny-ante. He had never been arrested, or proven guilty of any charges placed. It was luck or could have been labeled as something else.

"If that *cool-finger bastard* comes at you," Jeff assured, "he'll have to take all of us on."

Cedric was secretive about his mess; he felt like a ruler of females, and eliminator of males as needed. The town was his and everyone knew it. It was rumored that he had police, judges, lawyers, and other key players in his pocket.

Kirk and his boys did not fear Cedric—at least at a distance. He was no coward, but at times a good run was proven better than a bad stand. And, then he was not trying to live and die by the sword. Those guys who lived the hard life generally, did not have a bright future. No good woman with wide opened eyes would probably give any of them the time of day or night.

"Lori and the girls must think I've forgotten them," Kirk realized.

For him, a good talk with a long-time friend was very refreshing. Yet he had no idea their conversation had continued for more than forty-five minutes. Then, he remembered how it was, when they were energetic teens. They would just go non-stop, with this and that.

"Man we're working on our third drink," Jeff reminded, still wasting time with the Cedric drama.

Kirk realized that his buddy was right. They had gotten caught up in the safety and security of one's well being. After Jeff's time statement, he looked at his watch again. Sometimes the *ole tick-tock* was off by five or ten minutes. In any case, it was time to get back with Lori and the girls.

"How about we get together next week," Kirk suggested, finishing his drink.

Much had been discussed, and more would be put on hold. They were still in the dark about the murder of the missing guy. And it would not surprise them; if Cedric were taken in for questioning.

"That's good for me," Kirk responded, "call me, and I know I should watch my adversary."

The good fellows demonstrated a warming and brotherly-like handshake just before parting. Kirk looked over his shoulder as he left. Jeff remained at the bar with a few other buddies.

They watched Kirk with his cool and self-assured *I got this* walk.

"And you the same bro," Jeff gave a thumbs up.

"Everything alright," Rachelle asked. "You were gone so long we thought you got lost." She laughed at the very thought of it.

She had danced quite a bit, and decided to take a break. Her immediate thoughts were consumed with memories of Anthony. Rachelle could not get over the fact that Cedric actually resembled him, but in an odd way.

"You are funny," Kirk answered. "Jeff and I lost track of time. Good buddies do that you know." He sat with a curious look.

Jeff's message had struck a nerve. Kirk felt uneasy thinking about Cedric and certain things he personally knew about him. He was not one to spread rumors, and knew that keeping his mouth shut was the most sensible thing to do.

"You sure all is cool," Rachelle questioned again, "something deep is occupying your thoughts?"

Kirk just did not appear to be as he was before leaving with Jeff. She could sense that he was nervous and edgy. *What took place to cause him to do a 360?*

"Are you disturbed because Lori is dancing?" She wanted to know.

Kirk seemed to be in a daze. His mind was on his buddy's conversation, and how to counteract what just might take place later.

"No, not at all," he responded, "I don't have any claims on her; she should enjoy herself." Kirk was clear. "Then, I'm not that type of guy to dictate."

No way was he the possessive type. He believed in giving a person space, and likewise. After all, it never paid to overshadow the woman. He would leave that to Cedric, he definitely fit that mode.

"I will say," Kirk went on, "that although Lori and I may not have come here together." Then he paused long enough to add. "She has made it evident that we will surely leave together."

Rachelle was very pleased to hear him say that. It was enlightening, being in the presence of a guy who knew how to enjoy himself, and not act like a fool because his lady-friend was enjoying herself. But Kirk had no real cause to be concerned; Lori was interested in him only.

"Your friend seemed to be nice," Rachelle commented. "And thanks for the drinks." She was very appreciative.

"No problem," Kirk said, "it was Jeff's courtesy. He thought you were *hot* and beautiful chicks. He wouldn't allow me to foot the bill."

Kirk's good friend was not showing off, he was just a nice guy.

"Since we are on the question and answer page," he mentioned, "what's up with you and the saxophone player?" He was quick to add. "He's really after you."

"I'm not interested, as you may have seen," Rachelle assured. "He thinks he's all that and more. In a way he reminds me of someone who was once special in my life."

She didn't want to go into details. Kirk was a stranger, they had just met. Her motto was to not reveal your personal business at first mention. For a brief moment, Anthony, her *MIA* (missing in action) ex came to mind; although she had not seen him in years; then somewhere hidden within, her feelings still lingered.

"He's persistent, will not give up until he has you in his grips," Kirk was clear.

"Don't worry," Rachelle smiled. "I can take care of myself, and if I need help, you'll be the first to know; that is after my girls." She seemed calm.

The musicians evening ending number seemed to go on and on, before Lori finally returned from dancing, panting from lack of breath.
"I was about to come out there and get my woman," Kirk joked.
"Oh really," Lori responded. "Why didn't you?" She was comical.
Lori liked the funny phrase *my woman* that he used. She understood it to mean that he really did like her. That possibility held such promise.
"I didn't want the *no-dancing* guy to feel bad; he was struggling to keep up with you," Kirk looked devious.
That was an understatement, because there was a time that he too could not dance well. After hanging out with a couple of siblings, his foot-work improved. He could sincerely sympathize with Lori's dance partner.
"Lisa must be on pills or something," Lori mused, "she's still out there. I feel sorry for poor Jerome."
This was great; they were having a ball, and Kirk was a winner. He kept an eye on Cedric as promised, not letting this prevent him from enjoying the night with his new found friends. Jeffrey was right; Kirk was a lucky one, and the guys were envious.
Then Lisa and Jerome made a good pair. They were like hand and glove on the floor, moving in harmony to each beat. The evening match-up was almost perfect, with one exception—Rachelle. She was not in that kind of mood, but happy for her buddies.

PLAYBOY ON THE PROWL

The master knew what to do and how to do it, but it was not working on this chick. Cedric's reputation would be ruined if his home boys picked-up on it. He knew he was surely a natural. He never had a problem pulling women of his choice. Tonight was different for Cedric, though.

It was not normal for him to just try anything to reel Rachelle in with his bait. She would be a prize catch, not see it coming. He thought for a moment, hoping to construct a quick plan before the last set.

To him, *class* was Rachelle's middle name; trapping her would call for a more settled Cedric to emerge; special gloves were required for this female. This beauty was refined, giving the impression that she was a no-nonsense type woman. His perception: she would never fall for the tough rude approach. So the former, was a step in the right direction.

Cedric noticed her response to his stare; her eyes said one thing, but her demeanor, another. His body movements and manner, handling the saxophone, made it quite apparent that she was turned on. The smooth Jazz was an opening, warming Rachelle up to him. There was no doubt that this was a head start in a scheme to deceive her. Unquestionably, Cedric would pour it on during the next set. Time was money, and money was honey. *Mr. flattering* was the sole ruler of this game, and no dame was going to out-wit this lover. He was really determined.

Rachelle glanced at her watch once again; it was about time for the band to return. She could detect Cedric's nearness. Her peripheral vision was more than sharp, despite the conversation between Lori, Lisa, Kirk, and Jerome. Their chatter carried on without interruption. Rachelle was certain that ignoring Cedric—and focusing on Kirk's in depth explanation, why women were so into musicians—would ruffle the *player's* feathers.

Did he intentionally play the last selection 'Love Don't Love Nobody' for me? She really wondered. What a message to send someone you are trying to play.

She had seen it numerous times before. Cedric's game was the same—in a different disguise.

His poker hand would quickly diminish from a royal flush to a fold. Cedric did not know, but he was about to see, he was no match for Rachelle. Tonight the master would be exposed as a fake and the bullshitter she observed him to be. Time and experience had schooled her well. She had been there, done that.

Little did he know, he was the bait—not Rachelle. The plan was to have him eating out of her hand before long. She would call his bluff.

Then some time plans have a way of back-firing. Cedric's scheme was about to explode right before his very own eyes. *'What goes around; comes around'*. The guy was about to get a visit from himself. Rachelle would send his mail via special-delivery.

This playboy was known to be cunning; really skilled in deception. He was not one to back down from a challenge. It fed his ego when a woman played hard to get. Yet, he could tell that Rachelle would be difficult.

He went after her anyway. Cedric took it to another level…

For Rachelle, the night was still young. Who knew how it would end; in any case, she planned to enjoy while it lasted. She danced with Kirk's homeboys and others desiring.

Kirk found it funny. So now Cedric would have his hands full with other men who saw Rachelle as a beautiful and intriguing woman. After all, he didn't own her. Also, she barely acknowledged him due to his arrogance. Too often Cedric banked on his looks—and manner in which he entertained—to charm women.

From the female perspective, he was a knock-out. The *show-off* kept lots of money; drove a Mercedes, and really poured it on when a babe was with him.

The club owners loved when Cedric and his entourage patronized their establishment. The guy really knew how to make it rain (spending big money).

Some chicks shared the point about that type of guy; who they had an eye for. Lori and Lisa were curious about the *Cedric rumors,* whether true or not.

"Girl, the horn guy is handsome, but scary," Lori concerned, "we heard some for-real bad stuff about him roughing people up and worse."

"Made me shiver just listening," Lisa was alarmed. "And the way he constantly stared at Kirk and guys you danced with most of the night. Rachelle, I really think you should stay away from him."

And it was wise to heed such reliable information. Too many folk were saying the very same thing about Cedric. Rachelle's friends did not want her to get caught up with anyone or anything harmful to her.

They each had a point, and it was up to her to take notice.

"I agree," Lori frowned, "sounds like he is nothing but trouble with a capital ''T.''

"Don't worry," Rachelle assured, "I am not interested in *Mr. Slick;* he is the furthest thing from my mind."

She was very serious.

"Now, can we go to the ladies room," she continued, "my bladder is calling and I really need to answer."

They headed off laughing at her *wee, wee,* humor.

The restroom was packed. After hand-washing and checking her garments, Rachelle began refreshing her make-up next to a few ladies doing the same.

One bragged how the sax player winked at her, flirting; and another woman said he smiled at her each time, returning from intermission.

Boy! This was hot and interesting stuff floating around, and Rachelle's ears perked, gathering it. Still, another female thought that she had out done all the others; she boasted that he sent her his cell phone number by a band member.

Then she ran long excited fingers through a tight hair weave, fluffing the ends as if preparing for a photo shoot. She removed, from a black rhinestone clutch bag, a small clear bottle of what appeared to be perfume. Ms. Rachelle watched as the perky sort of female sprayed behind each ear and wrists.

Afterwards, she switched toward the door; and before exiting, turned her head in a facetious gesture, waving a hand; reminding others to erase any ideas they might have had of hooking-up with Cedric. One could say that she rubbed sufficient salt into the wound.

Rachelle, Lori, and Lisa waited for a response from the targeted listeners. With them there was only raised eyebrows and silence all about. The atmosphere was akin to a resignation unto defeat.

The unidentified woman thought that she had made an unforgettable impression on Cedric, and had high hopes of leaving with him. Then all of the women—except Rachelle and the girls—cleared the area, mumbling among them-selves.

"Well, I never," Lori emphasized. "What the hell was all of that?"

"You tell me," Lisa agreed. "*Miss Thing* really got her nose wide open for Cedric."

What an example of one putting all of his or her eggs into one basket. The woman had put a personal claim on a guy she thought was interested in her. That foolish misunderstanding happened all too often; and most of the times it ended with nothing really gained.

"Call it what you may," Rachelle submitted. "It sounds like hot-drawers to me." She giggled as she made her point.

"Rachelle you should be happy," Lori told it, "she's taking that shady one off your hands."

But her friend refused to comment. After all, Cedric was never in her hands, and not a problem to her. Rachelle would be troublesome to him and in every sense of the word. She politely rolled her eyes at her buddies, turning her head; then continuing to make a presentable appearance.

"You guys can leave," Rachelle said, "I will meet you on the dance floor."

"No problem," Lori puckered her lips, "I really need to get my moves on."

Both of them rushed out the door, heading back to their seats in a brisk strut. They would not be denied the opportunity to demonstrate how together they actually were. Any curious observers could see that; these were a pair of proud young ladies, out to make that perfectly clear.

I.M.O.L. (INDECENT MOMENT OF LUST)

Leaving the ladies room later, Rachelle noticed a shadowy figure in the dark corner of the hall. Walking slowly, she was cautious of her safety options, if needed; she was shocked, when she recognized Cedric's silhouette. And there he was, casually perched against the wall, grinning like a Cheshire cat.

He pulled her close unexpectedly; and before she could react, he began caressing and kissing the startled woman. Rachelle struggled for breath, reeling from the long and passionate embrace. She was appalled that he was following her like a dog in heat. Her mind said one thing, but her body another. With great intensity, Cedric's lustful look pierced her surprised body throughout. Although Rachelle felt like putty in his hands, she tried to resist.

"Baby, I want you," he whispered, "I know you feel the same." He was hoarse, putting his lips closer to her ear.

Rachelle was spell-bound and speechless; yet her slender body yearned from a hapless physical want and need.

"You don't want me," she managed. "You want any woman you see in here tonight, that you can get." Her response was believable but she was weak.

"Been watching you all night," he tried, "my eyes are on you and you only." He sounded rather convincingly.

But Rachelle was not buying Cedric's lies. She had just overheard three women talking among themselves about his flirting with them. She knew his game all too well. But Cedric was not taking no for an answer. He felt Rachelle's bodily reaction to his seductive rubbing against her; she was no doubt excited.

Naturally, his suggestive moves may have been more persuasive in another setting; but for now, he was scrambling for whatever his unsolicited advances would somehow allow.

Not again, I cannot let this happen again in my life. She sternly admitted to herself.

Rachelle's feelings surfaced that she had not felt since Anthony, the father of her two children. Cedric's soft and warm kiss reminded her of him. The way his eyes spoke without words. And his embrace sent mild electric shocks through her enticed body. Her eyes closed tightly in that flash-back moment; a relentless Cedric was Anthony right now.

Rachelle's mind took a hazy right turn. After all, she and Cedric were still total strangers. But she had no intension of letting the heated moment get out of hand. Yet she had to confess, that part of the desired passion their bodies hungered for would take over. It was a game to him; racking up women's hearts like one would on a pool table.

But for now, Rachelle would yield control to Cedric. Then she wanted to know what he was working with. The beast in him would be tamed in time; and she would do that slowly but surely. She had to concede, his lips and warm hands excited her—as Cedric fondled her breasts.

"This is just a sample of what I want and can do for you," he spoke softly; skillfully placing his hand under her dress.

Cedric circled her thigh, traveling to a private body area; it throbbed from a lasting touch. A sexual craving consumed Rachelle now. She needed to stop Cedric. He was about to lead her to *the-corner-of-no-strings-attached*. But she forced herself to get a quick hold; Rachelle grasped his wrist, pulling Cedric's hand from forbidden territory.

My body is trembling as though a wind storm passed by. She told herself. *I must not show him any reactions other than my determination to get out of his reach.*

A signal saved her from a quick sex fix; the keyboard player's musical notes, was an instant cue for Rachelle's rescue. The band's break was over.

"Don't leave," he pleaded, "I need to talk with you." Cedric wiped his dampened forehead with a large white handkerchief. He hurried back to his place on stage.

Rachelle enthralled, perspiring and quivering, made her way back to the restroom. As someone who was supposed to tame another person, she had not done a very good job at this telling point. Her satin under-garments were notably moist from the excitement of Cedric's sexual advances—then much more.

She searched her oversized handbag for facial tissues. There was a time when she carried reserve panty shields (used whenever she over exerted herself dancing); but there were none tonight. So the harsh paper towels and industrial hand soap would have to do. She needed to freshen up before joining the girls. Cedric had won round one.

"Well, what were you doing in there so long girl?" Lori wanted to know.

Here it comes, the third degree from my girls. She was still heated and had nothing convincing to tell them, in reference to any potential questions. And there were some. But before Rachelle could think of a response, there was more to address.

"Yes, I was getting concerned," Lisa was sincere.

Rachelle was still at a loss for words. She could not shake the lust-filled encounter with Cedric; it brought back too many memories of Anthony.

"I just needed to freshen up and think out some things," Rachelle said finally. She did not want to go into detail. But the evident scrutiny from the looks of Lori and Lisa confirmed that girlfriend was not believable.

"Well, I say lets hit the floor and let it flow," Kirk suggested. He assumed that the abrupt interrogation could go on; so he quickly decided to change the picky mind-set of Lisa and Lori.

"You guys go," Rachelle waved her hand in dismissal. "I want to sit this one out."

She calmly took a seat, watching them, head cheerfully towards the floor. Her legs were weak from physical excitement Cedric had brought on. She dared not make eye contact with him. Rachelle directed her attention to the dancers, still finding it amusing; the manner in which some of them demonstrated moves.

Before long, she was in deep thought about Anthony. They had met at a friend's anniversary celebration back then. He was very friendly; and catered to her the entire evening. Anthony did not come on to her, but charmed with seemingly endless and sweet compliments.

At first, they talked about so many interesting things; that Rachelle felt she had known him forever. She loved how his lips shaped during smiles. The way his eyes brightened in their deep conversation was also attractive. Not to mention, his pretty white teeth.

In all this, Anthony did not inquire about anything personal. Then he allowed Rachelle to express herself comfortably. And he was a good listener and detail observer; which was very impressive. Surprisingly, when she was ready to leave, he walked her to the car; saying goodnight, before returning to the party. Anthony looked over his shoulder, waving as she drove away.

Rachelle was impressed by his adorable demeanor. Most guys would have initially wanted telephone numbers, address and the works. But he was a real gentleman as far as she had noticed.

A couple weeks later—to her complete surprise—Rachelle received a call from him. She was a little puzzled as to how he had obtained her telephone number. As it turned out, a friend, after much insistence of Anthony; gave in and supplied the wanted information. But that was not before, warning him to treat Rachelle right; they were good buddies.

In time, it felt like an eternity to Rachelle before their first kiss. Ironically, the few guys she had gone out with wanted kissing during the first date.

Was there such a thing as being too much of a gentleman? She wondered. It was not that Rachelle did not appreciate him being respectful and all; although there was slight concern, as to whether he might be bi-sexual—or whatever. But then she dismissed that nonsense rather quickly. Then too, there were no clear signs to support her suspicion.

So as time went on, they became a lot closer and much more personal. Anthony had shared that he was an only child, with a really close relationship with his parents, more so mom. He would say that his mother had always commented how he and his father could very well be twins; were it not for their dynamic age difference, of course.

Anthony's dad was a busy man, who owned many businesses; and found little or no time to spend with his family. Things changed for him quickly and not all for the good. Anthony's future plans was to study law, but his father wanted to show him "the ropes" (ins/outs) of the family business.

So what could he say or do, he was still under age and had to obey dad's wishes. At a young age, Anthony was in for the shock of his life. As his father's business was unstable and in dire straits; mainly because he was really secretly a woman's man. Aside from that, he was a freewheeling big spender, and some other shady things that his son did not understand.

Dad was fairly good looking and knew his way around females—and a lot more. He looked much younger than he actually was; then so many unwittingly would say that Anthony might be mistaken for his father as he got older.

⁓

"Hello! Anyone home?" They were back, acting a nuisance; loudly calling her as if she were deaf.

"Rachelle, are you OK," the four questioned in unison. They sounded like a harmonizing group.

Rachelle did not realize how far in serious thought she had gone. So many things were resurfacing, then so confusing all at once.

"I'm just fine," she managed. That was before eager bystanders began to take notice of her loud mouth friends.

"All I can say is, that whatever it was that had you in such deep thought," Lori said, "should be put aside, girl." She was determined to at least investigate this later. "After all, we did come out tonight to have some fun."

Rachelle knew that there was a meaningful point to Lori's statement. Surely, she did not want to spoil the evening for them, by having flashbacks of the past.

"That's it then," Kirk said, in triumph. "Let's dance woman." He quickly pulled Rachelle from her seat. This time the band was really pumping up the music.

Cedric watched attentively as the two twirled around the floor. He could not understand why Rachelle had not looked in his direction since their heated encounter. There was no doubt in his mind that he had not gotten next to her.

Mr. Smooth's affect on her was not something she could have shaken so soon, he concluded.

Was he losing his touch or what? Yep, his work was cut out for him with this one. Already, she was mentally wearing him down, and it was disturbing.

"Anyone for a drink," Kirk wiped his forehead. "That last dance with you was just too much." He pointed at Rachelle.

This woman knew her way around the dance floor and could move like a feather, floating in thin air. Nothing was more spellbinding than watching a sexy female move gracefully to the music, knowing exactly what to do with each beat.

"I'm game," Lori readily accepted, "no harm in one more for the road."

Rachelle's nervous anticipation began to build. She felt that Cedric would make a bee-line towards her once the band quit playing.

Kirk summoned the waitress as the ladies talked among themselves, about the fun they were having and events which had taken place. Things seemed to be in synch, as the band finished their last selection. And in fact, so did Rachelle and the girls. They finished their final round of drinks, ready to call it a night.

As always, the three vowed to leave together, no matter what occurred; as far as any male counterparts were concerned. However, no one hurried to leave. The girls sat gleefully, making plans for the upcoming week; as the other club attendees said their good nights.

Once the crowd thinned, Rachelle, Lori, and Lisa gathered their belongings, heading toward the exit. Rachelle made no attempt looking back to see where Cedric might be. Kirk and Lisa's new found friend, Jerome, escorted the women to their car.

"Damn!" Lori was astonished. "He beat us outside to get at you Rachelle." There was disapproval in her tone.

They stopped in their tracks, looking at one another in disbelief. The guy was too bold, taking for granted and disrespecting the morals of others. It was a novel in itself, and how interesting it would be, seeing how it would all pan out.

Better still, it was combat, a duel between two people; each fighting in survivor of the inner-self.

"This fool got a lot of balls," Kirk turned to Jerome.

"I would call it a problem," Jerome frowned in response.

Cedric, ignoring the others, walked toward Rachelle without taking his eyes off her. He was not going to let her slip through his fingers. His reputation was at stake, and loser was not part of his M.U. (make up).

"I came out to put something in my car," he explained, "then decided to wait until you came out." He went on in uncertainty.

Cedric was not sure whether Rachelle would go for that lame excuse, but for some reason, he was really truthful.

"And," Rachelle questioned. Her hands were up. "What did you want?" She certainly was not pleased.

"Well," he went on, "I really wanted to speak with you, in private if that's not asking too much." He appeared nervous.

An otherwise moment of silence was rudely punctuated by the sound of crickets; the night air spoke its own language; and that took precedence. They stood with alert ears to Cedric's desperate plea to Rachelle.

I'm sorry," she said rather stiffly. "It's been a long night and I really need to get home."

Now was the time for show or tell. Rachelle was not in the mood to listen to Cedric. She needed an opportunity to hear herself think; not having her mind cluttered with anything.

"It won't take long," he edged next to her, looking at the others only briefly.

She looked at him in speculation. Rachelle hesitated deliberately, not uttering an immediate response. She did not want Cedric to think that she was one to hastily jump at his beck-and-call.

"Guys," she was confident, "wait in the car, this will only take a moment." She looked at Cedric with squinted eyes.

Rachelle could tell by her friends' expressions that it might not be a good idea to go even a few feet away with him.

"I'm staying right here," Lori was determined; folding arms across her oversized boobs.

It is better to be safe than sorry, was this woman's motto. Lori's interest affirmed that she did not feel comfortable with her friend leaving their sight with the shifty guy.

"I'll be OK," Rachelle assured. She promised to stay where they all could clearly see her.

"Make sure you do that," Lisa shouted. She made sure that Cedric heard what was said.

She was on the same page as Lori. There was no way she trusted her close friend with "Mr. Slick-As-Ice."

Cedric took Rachelle's hand gently in his; and led her a few feet to his car. He did not care to share the conversation with her nearby body-guards. What he had to say was for Rachelle's ears only.

"I just wanted," he gathered his thoughts, "to see you again. And spend some time with you." He really wanted to convince her; he was sincere. "You need to know that I am really not a bad person."

She looked at him, wishing that he were a mind reader, and to just leave her alone. Rachelle wanted him to find someone else to torture.

He could have had his pick of any woman in the club. Why bother her, she wanted to know. She was not ready to take off the battle gloves just yet.

"Look," she said, "you might be a nice guy." Her pretty face reddened with anger. "Who am I to say," Rachelle continued quickly. "I don't know you and really don't have the time."

She then turned, walking away abruptly. Cedric reached for her arm. He knew that the speed factor had best kick-in for him, or it may well have been over before it begun.

What the hell was this chick's problem? Most women would have given their phone number or numbers to him. But there he was, begging her for some time. The payback would be a b-t-h for her in due time if the occasion presented itself.

"Here's my card," Cedric tried to remain cool, "give me a call."

He held her by the shoulders, moving closer and wanting to continue what was interrupted near the ladies room. But this was not the time, nor place. There was no need to start anything with the fellows or her friends; they really meant what was said as far as keeping an eye on him. But to him, they were merely a bunch of peons.

He left her in bewilderment, but not before suddenly kissing her forehead. Then he slowly moved away. Still, Cedric wanted to give Rachelle something to think about. He could sense her watching each step. And there was hope after all for him, because at least she had accepted his card.

"Women," he mumbled, "always trying to play hard to get." He was so confident. Then he added, "I could write a manual that the brothers could use as a how-to get what they want and more from all of them."

Rachelle started back toward the car, past a moment of confusion. How to handle him; his arrogant and smart-ass-self would be no problem for her. In many ways, he was so much like all the rest. Cedric thought that he had it like that. But she would show him.

"H-m-m," she grunted, "and what was that all about? *He gives a kiss on the forehead like he's dealing with an adolescent.*" She was justly annoyed.

Tomorrow was a new day, and challenging as well. Which bridge to cross first, would surely be revealed. The choice was neither automatic nor simple. There were much less decisions to make, but this was not one of them. At times it could be rather difficult—just thinking about it.

INQUIRING MINDS

"What did he say?" Lori was not alone, wanting to know.

Her eyes were sore from straining to see through darkness. Then her mind was also cluttered with many questions, regarding what Cedric was exactly up to.

"It wasn't important," Rachelle said. She took a time answering. "He wanted me to call him next week," she added.

Hers was a vain attempt at presenting a fake smile.

Rachelle thought that she should have said a bit more to keep Lori from batting out more questions. Then she quickly got in the car. The girl on-the-spot switched to riding in the back seat; doing that would provide her with the subtle escape needed from Lori's inquiry. Her puzzling stare was also bothersome.

Then Lori and Kirk were still outside the car, embracing; as Lisa gave a soft goodbye to Jerome. Right after that, she sat on the front seat. Rachelle was pleased that Kirk kept Lori occupied longer than expected. Then again she was the chosen designated driver. Rachelle did not mind waiting; it would prolong Lori's picky interrogation.

"I want you to keep extra eyes on that guy," Lisa advised. "There's really something about him that makes me wonder about his intensions." Her stern warning was to be taken seriously.

Rachelle was truly relieved that, unlike Lori, Lisa did not question anything Cedric might have discussed; with their witnessing from a distance. He was like a jigsaw puzzle, needing to be put together. For some reason, Rachelle could not shake the fact that in an odd way, he still resembled her husband.

After Anthony's disappearance, she was sadly broken into so many bits and pieces. Her heart was shattered, not knowing how to mend it. Rachelle was at a devastating loss. She did not know that it was possible to love anyone as much as she loved him.

In their beginning, they were in their early twenties. That was their initial meeting together. He was her first. And that was all the more reason for deeply buried feelings; that she could not completely stop from resurfacing.

For Rachelle, it was never easy being a single parent with two children to care for. She herself was an only child, somehow alone in a *melting pot world.*

Her parents were killed in a horrific car accident involving more than a half dozen automobiles. It was around her twentieth birthday. Police reports verified that a group of teenagers on their way from a house party under the influence of too much alcohol, and other drugs, were drag racing.

And in their desperate attempt to dodge an oncoming tractor trailer, the intoxicated youngsters collided with Rachelle's parents' car. In that tragic mishap, their car flipped over into a mass of oncoming traffic upon the freeway.

Sometime later, the police were reluctant to give Rachelle full details because of the horrendous autopsy reports. It was reported that the car burst into flames after crashing into a number of automobiles. It was an uncontrollable highway inferno by the time emergency responders and paramedics arrived on the scene.

Rachelle's mom, dad and others were burned unrecognizably. Dental records were required to identify each corpse.

Her mother was survived by an only sibling, residing in San Jose, California. Then her dad had an older brother living in Houston, Texas. They both attended the service.

Fortunately for Rachelle, the funeral was not overbearing with a long and drawn out service. Many attended to extend their heartfelt condolences to the family. The late Mr. and Mrs. WynHurst were well known in their community.

They were dedicated advocates for the educational enrichment of youth and young adults. They found and funded The Mark and Danielle WynHurst College Scholarship Fund.

Later, it was a sure blessing to have Aunt Vera step in and take care of so much family business and in so little time. Rachelle's dad's brother, Gilbert, was of very little help with decision-making. However, he was more than generous when it came to offering financial support, if and as needed.

There was no question; it was a very painful time for each one of them. And just before his departure, Uncle Gilbert experienced an unexpected episode. Aunt Vera had gone to his room to deliver a personalized letter, left by his brother. Following a few soft knocks on the door, and with no response, she continued in a low voice, calling out to him. Finally, the door opened slightly; there he stood awkwardly, with his right hand behind him, holding the knob.

"Hey Vera," he said. "What's up?" The sound of sadness in his voice was rather heartbreaking. For a split second, Vera forgot why she was there.

"I didn't mean to disturb you," she replied, "I just wanted to give you this."

She extended her arm, handing over a long white sealed business envelope addressed to Mr. Gilbert H. Wynhurst. At the bottom left side in bold black letters it read **confidential**.

Vera had not really taken a good look at him until right now. There was so much that needed to be done; and time did not allow for a lot of any personal conversation. She had to admit to herself that he was quite a handsome hunk.

"What is it?" He wanted to know.

Vera heard him but did not respond immediately. She was too busy checking him out—from head to toe.

Remember, you just buried your sister and brother-in-law; this is not the time. She told herself in so many other words.

"I didn't open it, as you can see," she went on, "it's for you. I'll give you some privacy."

And with that said, she turned toward Rachelle's room; she wanted to make sure her niece was OK.

"Wait," Gilbert spoke quickly, "can you spare a few minutes?"

He gave the impression of being, perhaps, a lonesome man; only wanting someone to lend a listening ear.

Then he opened the door slightly further, allowing her enough space to enter. And with his right hand outward, palm face-up; he gestured for her to sit in the recliner by the window.

He took a seat on the edge of the king sized Victorian bed; dressed with a beautiful lavender comforter set. The matching pillows were satin and trimmed with pale violet tone laced ruffles. Although it was a very comfortable room, it was unconventional to his particular taste.

Gilbert was such a gentleman. So Vera sensed a certain warmth and tenderness in his presence. He was tall like his brother, about six-four; with salt and pepper mixed straight hair which offset his tan complexion. His proportionate stature complemented a weight; and she guessed that to be approximately two hundred and twenty pounds. Then she was really impressed with that overall assessment.

"I didn't want to say anything until Rachelle went to her room," he confided, "she has more than enough on her plate for right now."

He lowered his towering head in a moment of silence.

Vera was very attentive, wondering just what he wanted to share with her. Life had a funny way of bringing people and things together. Although, it could be so sad; that fact had to be somewhat of an untimely tragedy—especially in losing an only sibling. The road ahead would be rough, but together they would pull through. She understood that in time their sickened hearts would somehow heal.

"Six months ago," he continued, "my wife of fifteen years passed from cardiac arrest. There were no forewarning signs of heart problems. Her previous visits with the primary care physician, ironically, all showed that she was in very good health.

Vera's vocal cords went on lock-down. The words were there, but the usual soft sound had taken a break. Then without permission, her limbs went on auto alert control. It was as though they were programmed to react to another's plea for compassion.

She stood quickly, without realizing; found herself at his side, in an attempt to console her brother-in-law.

"I am so sorry Gilbert," she said softly, "I can't say that I know how you must feel, but I do know that *this too shall pass.*"

Aunt Vera wanted to hold him—close to her bosom, rubbing his round head, to hopefully lock out any pain that might consume a mourning body. However, she did place her arm around his shoulder, and began caressing his arm. It was merely an effort to demonstrate comfort.

Vera was also mainly appreciative, as a firsthand witness, that a man allowed his emotions to surface. Gilbert could not retain a rapidly rising river of tears. She had never seen any guy cry; this was a new experience for her. That old saying *I cried a river* was well founded now. Her brother-in-law's flowing tears were like an endless water fall. Plain facial tissues were not durable enough. She excused herself momentarily to secure a wash towel from the bathroom.

"Vera, please forgive me," he was very apologetic. "It's just too much for me to keep bottled-up inside."

Vera returned to her original place by the window. She wanted to give Gilbert enough time to get it all out, without any embarrassment. It was a wise decision, because she could see her solace getting out of hand; maybe turning into intimate acts of passion. At this setting, they were both vulnerable; he more so than herself.

After all, he had loss one love within six months of another. So *Miss Horny* and her *Love Jones* needed to chill. This was a time for comforting each other, but not in that sense. Her wanting body was just hungry for companionship.

"This is your moment," Vera said.

She was oddly grateful that Gilbert was so consumed with weeping, that he did not appear to know that she was *hot* for him.

"You are entitled to feel," she added, "no one's judging. Besides, it's not healthy you keeping so much locked inside without a release."

He wiped his face again with the soft towel; then reached for tissues, then proceeded to clear his nostrils. Afterwards, he looked at her with saddened red eyes; and without speaking, managed a thankful smile.

"I'm relieved to hear that you understand, and not take my actions as a sign of weakness. I really miss my mate. And now my brother is gone." Gilbert was sincere. Vera could detect as much.

"Mark and Danielle were meant for each other," he went on, "I miss them very much."

She knew that they would talk again, and hoped that it would not be by telephone exclusively. Her conjured plan was to have more personal time with the handsome man. In the meantime it took all that she had to keep her hands off him.

"Well, I better get back to packing," Gilbert said, feeling better than he did about half an hour ago. "I have an early flight. Promise to keep in touch."

"Well, get to it," Vera kidded. "Yeah, I still have a few loose ends to handle before my departure next week."

With that being said, he took a giant step across the room; reaching to open the door, watching her walk down the hallway. Vera's impression of her brother-in-law was that he was a loyal and caring individual; who like she and Rachelle, had many obstacles to overcome.

But how one may deal with grief is something that professionals felt they had a cap on. It was not necessarily true, because everyone has their own manner in which to hopefully cope with bereavement. There was no self-control to the limit of sorrow's duration. Actually, it was an individual thing.

"Knock, knock," Vera repeated before entering into Rachelle's room. "I just wanted to check on you before I take a shower and retire for the evening."

"I'm OK Aunt Vera," she said, turning down the volume on the television set. "I could not sleep; tired is the word and as you can see, nothing is helping."

Then, she reached out to her aunt who wasted no time, embracing her loving niece.

NEW ACQUAINTANCE

It took Rachelle a while to function without the presence of her beloved parents. It is said that time heals everything. Well, in this case, that remained to be seen.

Living in California was like a different world for Rachelle. Life was at a fast pace, and carefree. Then there were so many other things that made her somewhat uncomfortable. She was now in a strange environment. There was no one with whom to socialize, except Aunt Vera. Rachelle's friends and associates were in Delaware; and that was like being on another planet from where she was currently.

It was not unbearable, living with her aunt; she just needed time to adjust. Vera was a jewel though. She had not seen her niece since her sixteenth birthday.

For that occasion, she and Rachelle's mom had planned a surprise party. That special celebration was held at one of Delaware's very popular Open Table restaurants. The evening went well and Rachelle was really amazed about the great food. She also received some very nice gifts, and money envelopes. Those were yesterday's memories.

Rachelle had one year remaining to complete her Bachelor's degree; then she would continue on for a Master's in Criminal Justice. She had conducted her research of various colleges, before deciding to attend UCLA (University of California, Los Angeles).

Aunt Vera was very excited for Rachelle, because she too had attended the university; receiving a Master's degree in Political Science. She was also very instrumental in transferring her niece's credits, and without problems.

And she felt it was best for Rachelle to start the classes immediately. That would be good therapy in helping to keep her occupied. So in agreement, Rachelle did just that. The first day was hectic as expected; but by the end of the third week, she blended right in with the hustle and bustle of it all.

Rachelle soon made friends with a couple of classmates, Lori and Lisa. Sometime thereafter, the three of them became inseparable.

They studied, dined, and participated in activities outside of the classroom together.

There were still many times; the new girl in town thought about her parents. Rachelle knew that they would not want her to live life grieving their demise. They would rather she live it to its fullest. But in due time, it stood to happen. She would never forget the love and tenderness of Mom and Dad.

Although Aunt Vera was much more outgoing than her sister; in so many other ways she was a lot like her. The free-spirited woman was still a loving, caring, understanding, and very supportive stand-in-parent. There was no doubt that Rachelle was in good hands with her. She looked toward her well-trusted relative as an inspirational mentor.

Although Vera was gentle and easy going, she was also a statue of strength in Rachelle's mind. Early on, she had made a career choice to not have children. And that was not because she did not love children; she adored them. But 'V' (a pet name for Vera) understood the sacrifice one had to make in order to be a good parent.

So she made it clear to her suitors that a career was priority. Therefore she never accepted offers of engagements in hopes of marriage. Did this make her a selfish female? Not really. The well rounded woman knew just who she was, and what she wanted out of life. It could be said that she was very smart.

Rachelle had often wondered about whatever happened to cause such a clear-minded relative to make such a life-changing decision. But now was not the right time to question Aunt 'V' about her personal choices. They were still trying to cope with the loss of love ones who had passed on to greener pastures.

"What a night," Lori said, "there was not a dull moment, if I must say so."

The close buddies were all in tune to their own list of evening events at Deuce's.

"Girl, I feel you," Lisa agreed. "I had a great time; even met someone whom I feel may be worthy of my time."

Lori had broken the ice. Earlier she had turned on the car radio because the quietness was driving her batty. Then, she wanted to get some feedback as to what was on her friends' minds. For one thing, a puzzling Cedric's jive continued to eat at her.

If only Rachelle would say something. Then Lori would have an opening to question what he was so secretive about; with regard to her home girl, before they left the club.

But Rachelle did not bite. She sat in the back seat, and just too quiet for Lori and Lisa. With that silence, they wondered whether to leave her be for now, or try to get whatever they could from her later?

"Look, I know that at times I can be a real pain in the butt," Lori took the lead. "Our inquiring minds just want to know what Mr. Slick-Slick is up to."

She attempted to make eye contact with Rachelle using the rear view mirror. But her friend still did not utter a word. Lori reached across the front seat, tapping Lisa on the leg to say something. Then to her surprise, Lisa did not respond. She remained neutral. And Lori wondered what the heck was going on. Lisa usually followed suit whenever they wanted information from Rachelle.

Did they form an inquiring block-out against me? After all, she was the last to get in the car. Lori felt that her twit friends had time to form an allegiance to lock out the determined pursuit of questions.

Well, that did it! Lori did not intend to wait another second longer; to satisfy her curiosity. It was time to dig deep. The head-strong friend had a feeling she might just need hip boots before it was all over. But Lori had to go for it.

"Are you OK Rachelle," she asked. "You've been in another world since leaving Cedric."

Then Lori held her breath for what she felt may be a thunderous response from the tight-lip friend.

"Everything's just fine," Rachelle stated.

Her intension was to not allow any open-end answers. Then that might give Lori the opportunity to really bombard her with questions. Although she knew that it would not distract her from being nosey. After all, they had been friends long enough; that most times Rachelle knew what Lori and Lisa was about to say, before they opened their mouths. Just thinking about it made her smile. Actually it was rather funny.

"Is that all you have to say?" Lori went on, "Just fine. What kind of an answer is that?"

Now Lisa was on pins and needles. She was not sure whether she wanted to hear Rachelle's response. Lori was acting like a mother hen, Lisa still remaining quiet.

"It is, what it is Lori," Rachelle's tone was stern."

"OK, so this is how you want to drag it out," Lori was really fiery.

Now it was a little too hot in the car for Lisa. She had to let them get it out. Then too; she had no choice, Lori was the captain of the vehicle. However, she did think about asking Lori to pull over to the side of the highway until she and Rachelle agreed to a truce.

"Are you silent," she went on, "because of that Cedric guy?"

Then there was no way that Lori was trying to start a verbal fight with her friend. Could she help it if there was concern for Rachelle's safety? Further-more, they always had each others' back and no *flat foot, smooth talking punk* was going to change it.

"I know that you guys mean well," Rachelle went on, "Let's just embrace the good time we've had together tonight. We will talk about the rest later." She was sincere.

Furthermore, it was such a great feeling to know whatever was confusing now; she would not have to face alone. *Mom and Dad, was right*; true friendship could not be bought. They are the song in your heart that express care, they are the moments that lift you when you are down, strength when you are weak. True friends are the rainbow when the world around you is dark; and encouragement when support is needed.

For Rachelle, Lori and Lisa were all of those and more. They were the shoulders and ears when she needed someone to lean on and listen. Their friendship was like super glue. Surely, there was no doubt that it was unconditional.

Then looking back to this point; she could honestly admit that the happy times, surely out-weighed the not so happy ones.

"I think that's a great suggestion," Lisa said. She was relieved.

Rachelle had calmed the flame that could have developed into an out of hand battle of on-going questions by the two buddies. Certainly it was Rachelle's business and she would discuss it when and if she chose.

"You are so right Rachelle," Lori said, backing off.

"How about this," she continued, "I'm spending the night with Lisa. As you know, I have quite a distance to drive home; and don't feel I should take the chance, after drinking that last round of shots Kirk ordered."

Yes, Lori had really drunk a little more than usual; and so much dancing had surely worn her out. She could not wait to get from behind the wheel. Driving was making her sleepy. Fortunately, they were about a block from where Rachelle lived. Then, it would only take 20 minutes to get to Lisa's. Usually the route to her buddy's home took maybe 45 minutes, but at 3am in the morning, traffic was light.

"We can have lunch tomorrow," Rachelle suggested getting out of the car, "that's if you girls are up for it."

As they pulled off, Lisa put her head out the car window, waved good night, and shouted to Rachelle, "it's a date."

That night, Rachelle took a well needed long hot shower before retiring. Sleep did not immediately take over as she had hoped. Visions of Anthony and Cedric danced in her head, before drifting off into la-la-land.

I REMEMBER WHEN

Saturday, it seemed, came a little too soon. Rachelle did not really feel like moving from the snugness of her bed; wanting to remain under the soft, warm and comfortable baby blue ruffled covers.

But she had to get moving, before Lori and Lisa called; nagging when and where they were meeting for lunch. *I should have kept my mouth shut.* She thought after the fact. Now she decided that it would have been much better to make such a suggestion as that later on. *Well, the damage was done.* Rachelle had more to add.

However, she would give them a call later with a change of plan. In addition to that point, it took much motivation nowadays getting started in the morning.

Although there were times when she was unable to sleep, Rachelle would just lie in bed; eyes closed, wondering whatever had happened to cause Anthony to desert his family.

Then she could remember, as if it were just yesterday; his reactions when the sonogram examination confirmed her pregnancy; and that it was a girl. He was going to be a daddy once again.

Now she could still feel his manly, but gentle grip, picking her up into his arms; spinning her around with much joy. They were oh, so happy. After all he was a great dad to Anthony Jr., his first born. At that time, the father was very proud that he was having a son to carry on the Meyers name.

"Anthony J. Meyers," he repeated over and over again.

To Rachelle, remembering their initial date now; was like the first real vacation that she took with Mom and Dad. The excitement was just too much to bear for a young girl.

It was a cool evening, at that time, around 6pm; on a Saturday. Anthony arrived with the top down; driving a big red two door, Jeep Wrangler. He appeared to be a nice guy, and did not blow the horn like some nut might do. Likewise, he got out of the automobile calmly, walking slowly up the driveway; to the front door. Then he rang the bell like a gentleman.

When Vera answered, he stood looking confident. With a hand extended, he gave her a beautiful bouquet of assorted flowers. A very nice first impression was made on 'V' right from the start. However, he handed Rachelle a long stem red rose.

Then immediately after introductions, he escorted his date to the car; opening the door, and waiting patiently, until she was seated comfortably. Rachelle was pleased that the temperature was not as humid as it was at the beginning of the week. It was just right for the occasion.

"I think my aunt likes you already," Rachelle smiled. "And I know that those beautiful flowers really sealed it for you."

Anthony looked at her most gently; with eyes so bright, that they sparkled.

"Cut it out," he blushed, "I only did what any decent guy would do." Then he really smiled.

"Thanks again for the lovely rose," she said softly, "It was a nice gesture; I love roses." Her pretty brown eyes gleamed.

She was relaxed. The young lady ran long slender fingers through her natural reddish brown hair; as the cool summer breeze caused it to playfully fly about her face.

Anthony turned on the radio; they apparently enjoyed the sound of some of the favorite artists. And that went on until they reached their destination.

"I've heard a lot about this area," she commented, "but never found the time to check it out."

Anthony was glad that he was the first to show her the beach; and a few other things that he imagined she would surely like.

"Well I hope you enjoy what I planned for the evening," he was hopeful.

Dining at the Santa Cruz Wharf, Rachelle ordered her favorite dish of seafood; and to her surprise, it was also his. Afterward, they walked the Santa Cruz Beach Boardwalk. That well known historic and romantic promenade was the only remaining large seaside amusement park; on the West Coast.

They took pictures in one of the photo booths. Then in spite of trying a few rides together—somewhat thrilling for Rachelle—the fun couple had such an exceptional time. The freshness of it all was absolutely fulfilling. Anthony even rented bicycles so they could ride along the beach front.

All in all, Rachelle's evening was perfect. The time that they shared, gave them the opportunity to really feel one another out. To her, he was one-of-a-kind guy.

Then later, a most interesting date ended with an appropriate kiss. It was soft and light on the lips, yet so befitting. And the tender contact sent her into a want-more-mode.

Yet haste makes waste; then being a lady she contained herself, not really wanting to rush things. The promising relationship they shared established solid togetherness. And that meant more to her than an intense heat of the moment fling.

Rachelle wanted to savor it all. Ironically the infatuated female, now walked on clouds. There were thoughts of what was maybe meant to be.

For many weekends thereafter, the two were like Siamese twins; if one was seen, so was the other. Theirs appeared to be a match made in heaven. Most of the people who knew them, would quickly agree that they were indeed made for one another.

Sometime later, Rachelle and Anthony were invited to his friend's *show me what you're working with* beach party. There the long-awaited inevitable took place; in that their first sexual encounter came to be.

During the excitement, nearing the escalated moment of arousal and ecstasy, they found that each were—virgins. However, they were so engrossed that when orgasm happened; it took them on a roller coaster to heights unknown. The big dip could have been described as a paratrooper's first sky dive.

Love was no longer in the air now; it had totally consumed these intimate partners. They welcomed it as if at a loss for oxygen. Their bodies blended together for the never ending plunge; it seemed like that. Then it was a trip—for lovers only—with a private reservation to this hot couple.

They were overwhelmed under the glow of the moonlight; there were joint reflections on the rippling waves of water. The two were totally exhausted, yet fulfilled. A calmness of shared sweetness was present. The stars twinkled and appeared to have composed a melody for two linked hearts. An intense feeling of affection encircled them, deeply. It was love defined.

"Are you OK," Anthony asked.

His cares was a tender passion; although that well-tuned body had never experienced such feelings. Something had taken control of him. It was scary, but he had not and did not want to resist.

"I'm fine," Rachelle responded.

She could not think of anything, more or less, at that time. Therefore he had to take over the lead, as she searched for what to say. And that was not a necessarily automatic or easy task.

Sometimes words are not required in order to speak. Body language could represent verbal communication as a convenient substitute.

These young lovers united together, could better soothe the heart—like a most relaxing body massage.

Their sexual venture was complete now; and time seemed to stand still.

They were as motionless as possible; not wanting whatever bonded the loving pair; to grant a rushed release. Being suspended felt good, as if simply hanging by an emotional thread; but that was alright—they had each other.

BIRDS OF A FEATHER

Rachelle's consciousness began to drift into sleep, but now she was in the twilight stage. Her head filled with many thoughts that Mom had shared about friends and memories. The loving parent could spot sincerity a mile away, so to speak. She knew whether someone was genuine or not.

True friends are special Rachelle, Mom would say. *You cannot buy them and if you do, they aren't worth a nickel.*

She really missed her parents, but knew that they were in a better place. *R.I.P. Mom, Dad.* Thoughts of them would never leave her.

Fond memories were the story book of her life. They allowed the pages of her being to either flip backward or forward. They brought about laughter as well as tears. At times they caused her regret, other times they gave cheer. Rachelle's mind took her on a memorable journey. She reminisced past events; and that treasure kept her love for Anthony locked away, safely within her heart.

Then Rachelle drifted off into a peaceful sleep; that is where the brain waves create long-term memory. Some call it stage three, the first stage of deep sleep.

Sometime later, Rachelle had awakened to the musical sound of the cell phone on the nearby night stand. With eyes closed, she scrambled to answer.

"Hello," she was partially awake. It was way too early for any calls.

"Who is it," she asked, wiping her eyes. She tried to get herself together.

"Who do you think it is," Lori yelled. "Lisa and I are really starving waiting on you."

Now Rachelle was coming around slowly. Being alert, she realized that her body demanded more rest before Lori interrupted.

"I am sorry girl," she apologized. "I must have dozed off again. It was my intent to call you guys by 10 am."

Then she glanced at the time on her cell phone that showed 12: noon. She had slept two hours longer than planned.

N. O.

"So what's it going to be," Lori was inpatient. "Are we still on for lunch or not?"

"Sure we are," Rachelle said, "but let's make it brunch instead. It'll give me more time. I'll be at Lisa's by 2."

Then she heard Lori call out to her over-night host. Rachelle's suggestion was fine with her, but she wanted to see if Lisa was in agreement.

"OK," Lori answered, "we'll see you then, and don't have us waiting."

Rachelle knew that Lori was not one to kid around when it came to their outings together. She was a no-nonsense-for-time person. Whatever hour was set for a particular activity; the serious friend made certain that the word was bond.

Damn Lori, who made her time keeper of our lives? Rachelle thought.

So she hurried to get dressed, not wanting her friend to burst a vein. At times, Lori was like a time bomb waiting to explode.

By 1:30, Rachelle was on her way to Lisa's. She would actually arrive 15 minutes earlier. She grunted.

Let's see what Ms. Clock Watcher has to say now. She told herself.

When Rachelle arrived, her buddies were waiting on the front porch, ready to go. Of course, Lori stood out with one hand on her hip, the other stretched out checking her wrist watch.

The choice place to eat was a tiny, but nice spot where there was little congestion. They really wanted to enjoy the food, and be able to chat among themselves without the listening ears of others close by.

Lisa ordered a salad with green veggies, tossed with dates, cheese, walnuts, and bacon. Lori chose Marmalade French Toast with turkey breakfast sausage. However, Rachelle was undecided. She eyed the menu two or three times before drawing a conclusion. Finally, she ordered the Farmer's Omelet with bacon, onions, potato, and Swiss cheese.

"Well," I'm glad you made up your mind," Lori complained, "bad enough Lisa and I had to wake you to get here, and then wait for you to take half the day ordering."

Was there no end to the *mouth piece's* bickering?

"Chill out Lori," Lisa demanded. "You and I had discussed what we might eat if Rachelle chose this spot." She looked directly at her friend, and shook her head disapproving her behavior.

Neither Lisa, nor Rachelle could figure out what had crawled up Lori's tail. Ever since Deuces, she had been in an uproar. Could it be the Cedric ordeal? If so, they really needed to clear the air.

Rachelle did her best to ignore Lori. She was looking forward to her meal, and was not about to let her o*le over-protective* friend spoil it.

She was very fond of the restaurant. The atmosphere was really cozy and complimentary drinks were offered. Then soothing acoustic music came along with the meal.

Rachelle felt, that once Lori put some food into her slim body, the girlfriend would be more tolerable, easing her attitude. She thought briefly about the words of a friend; who would frequently say, "You better ease-up off me; better still, give me thirty feet."

The guy was so funny with so many spontaneous quotes, here and there. Rachelle always thought that he had missed his calling; and should have been a paid comedian.

After the meal, the three indulged in enjoyable moments of reflection; the ups and downs—especially some of the other more memorable past events.

"Rachelle," Lisa started, "I remember how you shared with us about losing your virginity. You were so silly."

Sure she could recall that conversation, but it was not that way.

"What do you mean, I was silly," Rachelle inquired.

She looked at them both, laughing; Lisa was right, she was somewhat ridiculous.

"You were funny," Lori emphasized. "You didn't know what to do."

Rachelle was quiet for a moment. But she braced herself knowing that there was more to come.

"Of course I didn't know what to do or expect," Rachelle added, "remember, I was a virgin, unlike you."

The three laughed together as they did back in the day.

N. O.

"Oh girl, get a grip," Lori was cheery. "I was amused when you told me and Lisa that you and Anthony threw your clothes on the beach while doing the nasty. Then later, you couldn't find your under-garments."

Rachelle simply looked at the girls and shook her head. They were not missing a thing. How come they remembered all this stuff so long ago?

"Yep, that was too much," Lisa giggled. "You said that you guys searched and searched to find your drawers. Then Anthony saw your panties floating in the water."

"Girl, I was so embarrassed," Rachelle sipped on the Pink Mascota wine. "There we were running into the water buck naked, trying to retrieve our clothes before the waves washed them out of reach.

She remembered that time all too well. Some of the other guests at the beach party saw her and Anthony in the water without cloths; and they too began diving into the water. They thought that the two were skinny dipping.

"Yeah, Yeah," Lori remarked, "don't get off the subject of you and Anthony being virgins."

She just had to go there, Rachelle surmised.

"Did you really help him," Lisa asked. "You know, find the welcoming mat to your vagina?"

She wanted to confirm Rachelle's far out explanation. Curiosity had the best of her.

"Yes I did," Rachelle tried to maintain her cool. "I knew me and he didn't. The bottom line is that we got better with each time."

Anthony was just as awkward as Rachelle. They were like infants taking their very first steps.

"Rachelle, you should have gotten some pointers from Lori," Lisa pointed toward her friend.

"That's right," Lori agreed, "Flame is my name, love is my game."

The ongoing conversation of the friends was getting hotter and hotter.

"You guys know that I didn't sleep around," Lori was serious. "I had some pretty bad knocks, opening my heart to fools."

Lori had learned her lesson, and practiced it faithfully from back then on. Life for her now was how she wanted to live it. Learning to love, and know self, surely made a difference.

"Today is a new day for you Lori," Lisa was gentle. "But back then, you took no prisoners. It was put up or shut up."

It was true, but most of Lori's hardness was just a front. It was her way of protecting herself after two abortions. The first came from puppy love sex; the other from a rape by her mother's drunken boyfriend. The latter happened at the age of sixteen.

Her pain was more severe—from her mother not believing her—than the act itself. Either way was devastating for poor Lori.

"We surely have come a long way," Rachelle said. "I have a lot of respect for your father who took care of that bum."

In a soft tone, she expressed compassion for her long-time friend's very frightening experience.

After Lori's mother sided with her man-friend, the abused teenager called her father who had been separated from her mom for about six years; to fill him in with the scary details.

Lori went on with them, how her dad removed her from the mother's care. Then he beat the boyfriend so bad that he needed hospitalization. The man was fortunate that he himself was not injured or charged for the severity of it.

The father had also filed criminal charges against the child molester. Then the legal system eventually made sure he paid for his crime. The boyfriend was sentenced five to ten years of incarceration.

"It's good that we can find laughter with it all now," Lori assured, "but it damn sure wasn't pleasant at that time."

Those days had contributed to her being childless then; but today the decision was by choice.

Lori wanted to be the opposite of her mother. Was it too much to ask for someone to truly love her; a nice man willing to be a sincere and committed mate or spouse?

When that time came for her—whether it was fifty or older—then so be it. Lori was willing to wait for Mr. Right.

It was time to move the conversation beyond where it was. Lori certainly did not want old memory wounds to resurface. Her eyes began to water from the very thought of it.

"Remember when you found out that your brother was bi-sexual," Rachelle and Lori almost spoke at the same time. They directed the attention to Lisa.

"Yes, and I don't care to talk about it," she said quickly.

She seriously wanted to evade the subject. It was not very comfortable for her, but the girls had put her in the hot seat.

"Well girl friend, that's just tough," Lori was determined to keep it going.

Lisa felt that sometimes her buddy could be a real pain in the ass.

"Look Lisa," Rachelle intervened, "all of that is behind you now. We aren't judging, we're sharing and enjoying the moment."

She knew that Rachelle was right. It was healthy to let bygones be as such. Although it was devastating, seeing her brother with a man.

"OK, OK," Lisa went on, "I walked in on my brother twice. Once he was a guy, and the other time a female. Until I told you two, it was confusing, because I honestly didn't know what bisexual meant."

It was a rather difficult confession, and still painful for her to talk about. The one family member, who truly understood, was always in her corner. When Lisa and her brother talked or had their own private family outings; it was like hanging out with a non-existent sister.

"After that incident," Lisa looked away only momentary. "I could not face my brother. Not because I was ashamed, but because I could not be there for him. I was not educated at all about such things."

"I'm sure that must've been a shock attack for you Lisa," Rachelle sounded sympathetic.

Lori was quiet for once. She crossed her legs and poured more wine into the glass. Then she took a few sips right before speaking.

"It was," Lisa confided, "but eventually I got over it. Deciding to confront my brother about his sexual preference took a lot of nerve on my behalf."

For more than a week, Lisa debated internally over how to approach him; and what she might say. There was always a chance of her being lost for words. So she decided to wait until they were alone. Eventually that opportunity came.

"I just went to his room," she continued, "knocked before entering, and asked him outright, what the hell was he, man— or woman."

She had hoped this would be it with all the questions. Even now, it was too detailed to continue.

"You told us that your mouth was opened so wide," Lori interjected, "that he could see your tonsils; when he explained that a bisexual was a person who is sexually attracted to members of both sexes"

Then Lisa's brother had dropped a more revealing bomb back then. He was not bisexual, but a hermaphrodite. Her brother was born with the sex organs of both male and female. Way back then, only the mother was aware of her son's unusual physical anatomy.

Then much later, the father was made aware of his son's decision to seek medical treatment by professionals; taking the necessary steps to become a woman.

Lisa could not comprehend why he would choose to be a woman and not a man. He wanted her to know, his reason for deciding to become a woman was because it was the dominant characteristic. Her brother assured her that nothing would change for them, because he would always love her. Then he tried to add humor to the situation by declaring that he would be more compassionate as a female.

"Sis," he began, "you know women are more loving than men, they are loyal in commitments and when they care, it's no half stepping; they give their all one hundred percent."

In order to fulfill the desire to transform to a female, he wanted to relocate once the operation was over. He had promised to keep in touch with his baby sister. Then they embraced as siblings for what seemed like an eternity. She really loved him. Lisa would surely miss his *blood thicker than mud* jokes.

Lori handed her some tissues. Then Lisa wiped away tears that trickled down her face. She assured them that she was alright, filling the glass with more wine. As soon as Lisa drank the first one straight down, another one came.

By now everybody was feeling the effects of the Moscato. The Q&A session was spirited by the sweet pink wine. The brunch held its own against glass after glass of the intoxicating grapes. The soothing music performed well, relaxing any tension that may have otherwise stressed them out.

Overall, it had been a rather productive "party" of old pals. The total atmosphere had lifted their girlie experience to another level. The afternoon get-together was just the food these chatty chicks had longed for—and really needed.

MIND GAMES

After dropping off her buddies, Rachelle headed home with a full stomach and a buzz from the alcohol. It felt good not having to worry about finding a place to park. She had a very nice home with a two car garage. So she was relieved for not having to find a place for her car.

Her single family residence was located in a cozy cul-de-sac allowing her to enter the home from the garage, if she chose. But for some odd reason, she used the front door that night.

Leaning against her door was a long narrow green box tied with a beautiful large red bow. *What could this be? Do they have the right address?* Rachelle figured that it had to be a mistaken delivery. *This for me, really?* The attractive box looked familiar. But she did not know anyone who would send flowers.

Still, she took the package inside where more light was needed to read the attached card. She removed it slowly from the envelope, only to find that it was addressed to Ms. Rachelle WynHurst. She further questioned who would send her roses.

The note did not reveal the name of the anonymous sender. The long stem red roses were beautiful. How nice of someone to think of her in this manner. Then too, the rose was her birth flower. The lovely gift was delicately placed in a vase.

Rachelle called the girls. They always did that whenever they had been out together. That was to let each other know that they had made it home safe. But there was no mention of the roses, at least at this time. Or *maybe later,* she thought.

The remainder of the week would be filled with conference calls; also meetings of the minds. It was all for a new project she had proposed to the sales department.

After her shower, Rachelle decided to record the events of the day before retiring for the evening. Keeping a journal was something she had started as a teenager. It was a relaxing endeavor that gave her freedom to say what she wanted and how. It was like talking to a silent friend. It was interesting going back to various dates, and being amazed by what she wrote.

N. O.

The day had passed quickly. It was 10pm. Usually during the week, she did not call it a day until around twelve, midnight.

Dear diary, today we reminisced. Some things were pleasing to recollect, while others were not. I am truly blessed to have genuine friends like Lori and Lisa, and two wonderful children. I continue to miss Anthony, and know that my love for him will never fade. I know that Mom and Dad are watching me from heaven. Chow! ME, Rach.

She always ended her journal recordings with at least one pseudonym. Rachelle smiled as she thought about her sister-friends Lori and Lisa. They were very special to her and the bond they shared was sealed really tight.

Then she nestled between the soft, smooth sheets, and welcomed a sleep that came right away. Unfortunately, her instant unconsciousness did not block the sound of a suddenly loud then constant ringing telephone. Being half asleep, she reached for the receiver.

"Hello, hello," Rachelle repeated, but there was no response.

She glanced at the clock showing 2:30am. Wondering who might call at that hour; she dismissed it as a wrong number. Then Rachelle hung up and drifted back off to sleep.

It had been a long day. Her body ached from so much laughter. Plenty of rest was what was needed.

She awoke well rested. And before starting her day she had breakfast. The early meal consisted of a heated blueberry muffin and a cup of decaf coffee.

Now she was ready for her first conference call which was difficult to keep as just that. She never looked forward to dealing with the CEO at the New York branch, because the guy was always trying to turn the business discussion into something sexual.

Rachelle had met him in person twice, and that was one too many times for her. Once he had scheduled their meeting at a hotel conference room; that was more like a suite. But it was not an appropriate place for a meeting.

After it adjourned and just about everyone had left; he convinced Rachelle to stay and discuss another proposition. He needed some credible feedback regarding the latter, before presenting it to the team. It sounded like a good idea.

So naturally, it was in her best interest to honor the suggestion. It could have meant killing two birds with one stone. She wanted to seal her company's deal and another which he continued to drag his feet with.

However, Rachelle was strictly about business, but he had something else in mind. During the discussion, he changed in mid-stream. It was no problem for him to let her know that he wanted to sleep with her. For him, it was not a big deal, because most of the women she worked with had obliged his wishes.

Rachelle's private name for him was *No Name*. He outlined what he liked, such as being spanked, he wanted her to dress him in a bra and girdle. The man wanted her to make-up his face and apply lip color.

This fool is sick, she said to herself.

Rachelle was a step ahead of him. She had heard that he was weird. He could be handled, but first she needed him to sign the contracts she had on her person.

The guy was a sexual sadist. It was unbelievable, how he was aroused by the things he wanted her to do. Beyond help was the diagnosis because he could only get it up by someone inflicting pain upon him. Then surely his wearing women clothing was humiliating to her—not to No Name.

Rachelle excused herself for the powder room. She required a little time to tend to small private matters. As a woman, that was her absolute right, whether the gesture was bona fide or bogus. Girls like her were too much of a lady to let on to whatever they decided to do in the ladies room. It was their sanctuary.

Shortly she returned ready to get it over with. Rachelle poured drinks, slipping a few sleeping pills in his glass. Then she pulled out the contracts, giving him an ultimatum. She gave him the impression, that pleasure awaited him only after he signed the papers. It was a teasing ruse.

N. O.

He could not get to his pen fast enough. It was all too easy for her, she could plainly see. Then they boarded the elevator.

The room was an executive suite; fresh fruit was placed in the center of a round table. A lovely arrangement of assorted flowers was also displayed. And the bar was fully stocked. The atmosphere was such that one would be enticed to extend their stay. That is, if they could afford it.

By the side of the bed he opened a suit case that housed the items for the night. He wanted to watch Rachelle undress, but her plan was to only remove her blouse and skirt, leaving him to settle for the body suit she wore. Her under items were sexy, and expensive. The snug fitting piece was laced smartly around the breast area, with black satin material that made up the rest of the garment.

She could tell that the pills were beginning to take effect on him. So Rachelle quickly poured another drink, handing it to him. He took a few sips. Then, she removed the items one at a time. He was anxious to put them on. The sick puppy was particular about the shade of lip stick he wanted to wear.

Cell phone pictures were in order when she finished. The photos were her protection against any lies he might tell others later. It was not blackmail, only a precaution.

She had given him enough pills and drinks to keep him out until later the next day. No Name had passed out reaching to feel her buttocks. Rachelle pushed him onto the bed, where he fell with his legs spread wide. His arms were stretched out, looking like a scare crow on Halloween.

The deals had been sealed. So with a job very well done, Rachelle was later offered a partnership with the company. *Great!* To her it meant a much better salary. And she deserved it for the hard work. Her diligence had paid off. She was one of the original employees who committed time and effort to get "This Style for You" off the ground. It was a pilot company that Rachelle and the others believed in.

After the call with No Name, she took a break, made a salad, and ice tea. She did not want to stuff herself. That would only make her want to take a nap.

But before she could enjoy her meal, the bell rang. Rachelle opened the door to find a delivery boy standing there with another box like the first one in his hands. He smiled as he handed over the flowers.

"Can you please tell me who they are from," she requested.

She wanted a favorable answer. Rachelle did not appreciate the mystery attached to such a thoughtful gift.

"Sorry miss," he answered sheepishly, "the manager instructed me to deliver to this address."

Now there was really cause for concern. Rachelle began to feel very uneasy by it all.

"A trip to the florist should clear the matter," she proposed.

The rest of the day went rather well. Then the remaining calls were simple and did not require much attention. It was 3pm and she had finalized some long out-standing contracts. Rachelle loved her work; it allowed unlimited flexibility and freedom.

Lori and Lisa called almost daily, usually around 4. Yet it was 3pm and the telephone rang. She picked-up instantly.

Well, she anticipated, *they are about an hour early. Wonder what's up?*

"Hey guys," she answered, "why so early?"

Once again, there was still no reaction on the other end. So Rachelle instinctively dialed Lori's cell number.

"Hi girl," Lori said, "what's wrong? You couldn't wait for us to call you?"

"No, that's not it at all," Rachelle let it be known. "Something's not adding up, and I need to talk to you and Lisa as soon as you get off from work."

Lori sensed some concern in her friend's tone. She began clearing her desk, needing to leave ASAP.

"You got it girl," Lori assured," I'll call Lisa and we'll be there around five."

It was a relief to have friends whom she could count on. Rachelle's first thought was that the call might have been from No Name, trying to psych her. But he was ruled out. Anyway, the embarrassed pervert did not want any further dealings with her; other than work related matters. After the hotel ordeal, he was very careful to avoid her.

Later when Lori and Lisa arrived Rachelle was all nerves. She had drained her brain trying to determine who sent flowers. The calls were also upsetting.

"What's going on?" Lori asked. She did not want to wait on Rachelle.

But her behavior was out of the norm. Something had the otherwise calm woman on edge; and that was causing concern.

"That's what I want to know," Lisa frowned. She was confused.

What was so urgent that she needed to see them right after work?

"After I dropped you off from our brunch," Rachelle went on, "I came home to find roses at my front door. Soon after, someone called me, but did not answer."

The girls were bewildered. And for a moment, none of them could imagine who it might be.

"Do you think it's the freaky guy?" Lori threw out a likely suspect.

Someone was playing games on their girl, and it needed to stop.

"No, he's been ruled out," Rachelle confirmed.

No Name, absolutely wanted no part of her. He still knew that she was not the one to fool with.

"Honestly Rachelle," Lisa was nervous, "I think it could be that creepy Cedric. I said it once and will say it again, the guy makes me uncomfortable."

Just who in the hell was Cedric? They had met him at Deuces and now he was a thorn in their side. Lisa did not trust him then and she sure as heck did not now. She was not putting anything past him.

"You know Lisa could have a point," Lori agreed, "I'll bet my last dollar it's him."

Cedric was just a thug in designer suits. But then sooner or later his hour glass would surely empty. He had the ability to camouflage whatever he actually was.

Then sometimes the truth could not be hidden. The shaky guy was just dishonest. He simply did not appear to care about anyone or anything, except himself. There was an air of arrogance that had the buddies disliking him.

"If it happens again," Rachelle referred to the flowers. "I'm going to refuse the delivery. And if they are left while I'm out, I'll personally take them back to the florist."

Now it began to sink in that it probably was Cedric. She had called about the puzzling matter in hopes of getting the name of the sender. But there was no result. Whoever it was, the person wanted to remain anonymous. After all, *the customer is always right.*

"You do have caller ID don't you," Lori inquired, "pull the name and number from the incoming call directory."

She looked at Rachelle only briefly, who appeared to be searching for some answers.

"I do," Rachelle said, "but the call shown is unlisted."

"Well if it is *Mr. Slick*," Lori responded, "we will find out sooner or later. I hope it's soon."

She was really pissed. She had had more than enough of the dumb pranks.

They decided to call Lisa's friend Jerome. Perhaps he and Kirk could offer some assistance. Meanwhile, Rachelle planned to resist answering the unknown calls.

There was some rather sweet then incredible stuff happening here. Mysterious flowers were a most thoughtful gift—from whomever.

Rachelle was just a regular girl; and they all enjoyed a beautiful bouquet. But whether they were from the "main man" or some "secret admirer", the sender was expected to at least step-up eventually, and become recognized. A caring male emerging from behind the curtain of secrecy was an enormous gesture. A worthy girl would appreciate the roses even more, once the man's identity was revealed.

At that time, perhaps, the receiver and sender could carry a great idea further. It was just that simple.

N. O.

But receiving phantom phone calls was from quite a "different place" than embracing long stem roses. The world was full of creepy characters. So a woman could not be too careful. A call without a caller breaking the silence—when on the receiving end there was a "hello?"—was an issue of concern. It was quite normal to pick-up on a, "Sorry, wrong number." As a handy apology, that was a reasonable explanation. Then a muted caller was always something to be concerned with. She knew that upfront.

FAIR FOR THE GOOSE

The flowers and the calls continued, and Rachelle stayed true to her word. She refused each delivery; then returned others. But what was happening had a name. The fact was: someone was stalking her. And it <u>had</u> to stop.

To this point she had not involved her children in this ongoing madness.

Lori and Lisa wanted her to involve the police. Surely they could help get to the bottom of this nerve wrecking dilemma. But for now, Rachelle decided to put it on hold.

By the end of the week, she had come up with a plan. She would rent a car and the three of them would follow Cedric. It was time to take action. The girls were raring to take part in the under-cover plan.

So they waited until Friday, Cedric's night to play at Deuces. They planted themselves out of sight; watching closely for him to leave the building. They did not have to wait long. He came out, got in his car, and drove off.

He stopped at a service station for gas; then proceeded towards the far west side of town.

After about an hour's drive, he pulled up to a single family home and went inside.

"Now what," Lori asked.

This certainly made her jumpy. *Suppose he had seen us tailing him.* The three of them would have surely been mince meat. It was feared.

"We wait awhile," Rachelle instructed, focusing on the house.

She had pictured Cedric living in a mansion, maybe. He certainly gave the notion that he had it like that. But this location was simply mediocre according to her observance.

"What's a while by your time table," Lisa asked, wanting an answer.

It seemed that their private eye scheme had come to a halt. The wait was shorter than expected.

As Cedric reappeared, carrying a silver attaché case; they slide down in the seats, fearing to be seen.

He put the case in the trunk of a different automobile. It was a custom made black Mercedes Benz. He soon took off and at medium speed.

"He's heading toward the beach," Rachelle observed.

During this time of night the beach was usually deserted. Safety restrictions were posted about to discourage illegal activities. The secluded place was also a well known location for gang initiations.

"OK," Lori pondered. "Who would be meeting him at 4 in the morning?"

Perhaps they were biting off more than they could chew. Suppose these amateur detectives were bait. He may have been aware of them following him. There were hopes that their plan would not backfire.

"Well, we will soon find out," Lisa assured, "whatever the reason might be, it's probably against the law."

Cedric parked his car, turned on the emergency blinkers, as if he was signaling someone. Then out of nowhere, a red convertible showed and parked next to his vehicle. The driver, a female got out, and went to the back of the car. Then a man in a white suit got out of the backseat of the Jaguar, joining the woman.

Rachelle, Lori, and Lisa watched as the pair opened the trunk, pulling out a body that appeared to be a male. His hands were tied behind his back and a black hood covered him, head to neck.

The chick in a red mini maxi dress removed the hood. His mouth was covered with gray masking tape. She pushed him toward Cedric, who then handed her the case. Then they drove away.

"Oh, my God," Lisa really feared. "What is he going to do to that guy?"

Suddenly, Lisa wanted to get as far away as possible. She was concerned about everybody's safety, including the poor guy.

They had a gut feeling that something was about to go down. And the friends did not want to witness any foul play.

"I don't know," Rachelle whispered, "but whatever happens, we certainly can't move without the risk of being noticed. So we'll stay here until Cedric leaves."

The shady man apparently had a job to do. He was about to put some time in on it. He removed a gun from his back pocket, what looked like a Baretta. Then he attached what appeared to be a silencer. Although they could not hear a word, Cedric was definitely saying something to him.

They walked to the edge of the beach. The guy had to be forced to make the short trip. This time of night the waves were choppy but euphonic. Then that precious peace was just about to be disrupted.

Cedric held the weapon against the man's head. The girls watched in horror; their mouths buried in hands.

As without hesitation, he shot twice, point blank: first in the head, then in the chest.

"Oh no," Rachelle exclaimed. "We just saw a man maybe lose his life."

Nothing could describe what the three were experiencing at this precise moment. It was as if their hearts were running for cover.

There was no doubt that their collective blood pressures had sky rocketed. Would they make it away from here alive? This was an instance of serious doubt.

"Girl, what are we going to do," Lori was in panic.

"Nothing," Rachelle said coolly, "there's one thing we will do, and that is keep our mouths shut."

She sensed that her home girls could not handle what they had just seen.

"Neither of you," she added, "can mention a word of this to anyone, not even the guys."

This had surely been a regrettable move. Her plan had led them to witness a life taken by the hands of a monster. Rachelle had to admit that Lori and Lisa were right to be suspicious of Cedric. He wound-up being nothing more than a cold blooded murderer.

Mum had to be the word, or else; because if he found out that they had watched him kill, he would probably not hesitate to eliminate them also. Rumors had it that Cedric had murdered many in the past. He was too powerful and never served any time for his alleged crimes.

"Well, as for the mysterious flowers," Rachelle said, "I know a couple of Private Investigators who are clients. I'll ask one of them to stake out the florist shop to see if they can come up with something."

It was a start in the right direction. But back-up was still needed. Things were a little too hot for them. If they were ever pushed into a corner, Rachelle would revert to a characteristic that she had secretly kept for a very long time. Now she was a different person. The other one was treacherous, dangerous, and damn right cold-hearted.

Rachelle did not have MPD (Multiple Personality Dysfunction), but she could still summon a few personas, if having no other alternative.

There were many times the usually cool headed woman had to do things that she was not proud of. But those actions were done for her survival.

Nowadays, it was a wonder how she got away with it all. But at that time, the shrewd female made the black widow spider look like the cartoon character, Cinderella.

"Right Sherlock," Lori wiped her face of a nervous sweat. "I suppose if that doesn't work, you have something else in mind."

Lisa really knew how Rachelle could be, once she had determined. The girl could be a *stone nut* whenever she had to.

They finally got in early around six. Lori and Lisa could not sleep, fearing that Cedric would find them out.

Rachelle took a shower and tried to get some rest. But the body had total control during extreme tiredness or fatigue.

The three spies were really beat, mentally and physically. They had been through quite a lot within the last twenty four hours.

The stake-out had not revealed Cedric as the flower sender. The helpful investigators had secretly gained access to the shop's files. They found that Rachelle's name and address for the deliveries were correct. Attached to her folder was an address for the sender. It turned out to be bogus. All the receipts acknowledged that whoever it was paid in cash.

Then as if it never happened, the flowers and telephone calls stopped. The girls thought that maybe the shop owner had alerted the anonymous sender to the legal inquiries made by the private investigators.

They were still on emotional edge. Rachelle checked the news papers and tuned into daily television news; but there was no mention of any dead bodies found at the beach. The waves might have washed it out to sea.

Still she watched her back leaving and returning home. Rachelle made the same suggestion to Lori and Lisa. It was time to move on. They couldn't put their lives on hold because of Cedric. He killed a man, not them.

The buddies also needed to remain cool; the way they were acting, the good guys might easily suspect that something was wrong with them. And truly, there was; but they did not have to advertise it to Kirk and Jerome.

Rachelle's friends were paranoid. But Lisa shared that it felt like the dead guy tried to pull her underwater as she swam. And Lori swore that she saw him walking on water. After that, the girls refused to return to the beach.

"We are going to need counseling if this keeps up," Lori confided.

She shook noticeably like a person with a drinking problem, and coming off a binge.

"She's right Rachelle," Lisa agreed. "Last night I almost knocked myself out running from my shadow. I just knew something was in my house."

They could not understand why this thing affected them so much. Then why not! They had never seen a murder—except in the movies or on television.

"So how come you're not falling apart," Lisa stared at Rachelle.

"Because we did nothing wrong," she said calmly.

Although none of them was insensitive to a human loss of life; being an eye witness had certainly changed them. It was not very frequent that three innocent parties got to witness a brutal act such as cold blooded murder. But they did and were smarter for not uttering a word about it. A large part of that decision was based on fear.

"I don't know why you are so surprised at what you saw," Rachelle said. "After all, it was you who opened my eyes as to how cruel Cedric could be."

A ruthless man such as him could easily rationalize the cold brutality of senseless slaughter. Sure, Cedric may have been a serial killer, but it had yet to be proven. The poor guy whose life ended on the beach could have at least testified that Mr. Executioner was in fact a one-time murder—himself being the victim.

Although a dead man could not bear witness, surely there were three eye witnesses who would beg to differ; were it not for their own lives possibly at stake. The frightened but smart girls' lips were sealed solidly.

Rachelle knew that no matter what, they all had to stick together. There was strength in numbers. They knew that too well.

"I got your back, everything will be OK." She swore.

SWEET AND SOUR

It had been more than a month later, when the local news reported that a body had washed ashore near the beach. The girls were relieved, hearing that the police had unnamed suspects in mind. Eventually, the case was closed and classified as gang related.

It took awhile, but things returned to normal. Lori and Kirk were deeply in love; Lisa and Jerome had their eyes on engagement rings.

For them, quite some time had passed since they had been to Deuces. The vote was unanimous; they did not care to ever go there again. That was providing Cedric was no longer performing there. The further they stayed away from him, the better.

So, every other Friday after work, they enjoyed outings at Club Notions. Rachelle was still the odd-ball, remaining dateless. But that did not matter. Lori, Lisa, and their dates wanted her to hang with them anyway.

It felt good, not having to fight off the wolves. She met guys, danced, drank, and had a great time. Then they went their way; Rachelle went hers.

Sometimes things were just too good to be true. All went well—until the night Cedric walked into the club.

"No, don't tell me," Lori was disappointed.

She felt they should have known the inevitable. Was there any where they could go without running into him? *Maybe we should just move to another state.*

"What Lori," Rachelle asked, "what's the problem."

Rachelle had just returned from dancing, and was having a friendly conversation with her partner.

"She's talking about that," Lisa pointed to Cedric.

Rachelle knew that he usually played at Deuces on Fridays. So what was he doing at this place? The shock of seeing him instantly turned their fun time into gloom.

"Why are you guys tripping," Kirk wanted to know. "He's human, not God."

He had noticed the quick change in their actions. The expressions the girls projected, was that of fear. They looked at one another suspiciously.

How wrong he was. Of course Cedric was not God; neither was he human-like them. He was a monster. It seemed that the harder they tried to get away from him, the more he haunted them. Their wishes for him to disappear were all in vain.

Although he was in the company of a female, he made it his business to approach their table.

"Hello Ms. WynHurst,' he greeted Rachelle with a crooked smile.

How did he know her last name? Very few knew other than co-workers, family, and close friends.

Thinking back to their first meeting; she remembered introducing herself by first name only. She did not care whatever he was; Cedric was not about to get away addressing her, using the surname.

"The name is Rachelle," she was cold, "if you don't mind."

He gave her a chilling look. But she was not afraid of him. If anything, he should get out of her face.

According to her past reputation, which he was unaware of, she could be just as cruel.

Then this became a stare down. Rachelle was not backing down from the *executor*.

"Not at all," he briefly looked away at Lori, Lisa and the others. "Then Rachelle it is."

And with that, Cedric and his entourage followed the waitress to the VIP section.

Soon after he left, there was an announcement that drinks were on the house, compliments of Cedric. Rachelle felt he was just showing off. This time, she would not refuse his generosity.

He eyed her every move as before. But this time, if her bladder called, she was not going to the ladies room alone. He would not catch her off guard again. Cedric had shown Rachelle what type of person he really was.

"How about we finish our drinks and get out of here," Kirk suggested.

He did not know exactly what that scene had been between Rachelle and Cedric. But he did feel that it was a bad sign, whatever.

The last person who publicly stood up to Cedric disappeared. Kirk really did not want anything to happen to Rachelle and the girls. One day that bully would get what was coming to him. It was only a matter of time.

"I'm with you all the way," Lori agreed. "The guy makes me nauseated."

Rachelle was quiet. She still could not shake the fact that Cedric looked so much like her missing husband, Anthony Sr. They finished their drinks and quickly left the club.

"So what are we suppose to do," Rachelle was upset, "leave wherever we are when he decides to pop in?"

She had no intension of running from the *Big Bad Wolf*. It was obvious that Cedric was getting his *'Jones'* off, through feeling that he intimidated them. He had managed to turn a wonderful evening into quite the opposite.

But all was not lost. They went to Kirk's place and ended their night with more drinks and laughter.

Kirk was a comedian at heart. He demonstrated a few martial arts moves that at times caused him to trip over his own feet. It was hilarious, watching the brother spin around, trying to maintain his balance. Then Rachelle thought how all those kicks and hand chops, would not be enough to dodge Cedric's bullets.

The following week Rachelle arranged to have lunch with her son and daughter. Anthony Jr. always prided himself on a fine choice of restaurants. He had good taste like his father, she would comment from time to time.

After they placed their orders, Antionette shared with her mom some very interesting news. She had been offered the opportunity by the university she attended, to complete her last year of study abroad.

"Mom, say you'll allow me to go," she was really excited and looking forward to a new adventure.

The young female was so elated. A change of atmosphere would be just great. And to be able to travel to an interesting country, such as Italy, was really more than what she could ever imagine.

"Sweetheart," Rachelle was surprised. "I'm very happy for you. But Italy is not like taking a plane to New York. It's so far away. And one year without you, would be like a decade for me."

Rachelle could tell that her daughter really wanted to go. After all, Antionette was not under age; she was old enough to make her own decisions. She was just being respectful. It was just a motherly instinct, not wanting to let go.

"Well Mom," Anthony Jr. tried to ease the tension, "you'll have me. I think it will be a great experience for baby sis. How often does one get a chance like this? Just think she'll be bilingual when she returns home."

Anthony sensed that it would be difficult for his mom, having to send her child off to some strange foreign country. Heaven help her; if Antionette was mesmerized by the mere essence of it all, and decided make it her home.

Even worse, she might fall for some Italian guy and get married. Those men were said to be really good romantics, and known for sweeping a woman off her feet.

In a way, the thought was funny to Anthony Jr. But he was sure that Mom would not find it so. Likewise, she would have a panic attack.

"Can we just enjoy our meal," Rachelle wanted to change the subject. "I promise we will talk about it before you leave for school."

She watched her children who were no longer adolescents. They were now adults who would always be her babies. The proud mother held much admiration for how they had turned out. Rachelle was proud of their accomplishments, and prayed that the future would be even brighter for them.

But all good things must come to an end. Then, not really, that was as if put in the context that nothing lasts forever. Her pleasured moment was short-lived. When she returned from the restroom; standing at their table addressing her children was Cedric, her nightmare.

"Hello Rachelle," he greeted. "I was just telling Anthony and Antionette about my band, and how I am now the proud owner of this establishment."

He waited for whatever she might throw his way. Soon and very soon she would be all his, he thought. She was putting up a good fight, but he would wear her down. His money was just that long. He could buy anything and anyone if he chose. Ms. WynHurst could not run far enough from him.

"Congratulations," Anthony Jr. said, "but do I know you?"

He did not appreciate strangers making like they knew him. Where did this dude come from? His face was familiar, but Anthony had never met the guy. Then he did not approve of how he looked at his mother.

"Not personally," Cedric answered, "but you are the new buzz around the court rooms these days."

Rachelle struggled for her voice. It had better come out of hiding quick. Who did Cedric think he was, interrupting her privacy and quiet time with her family?

"And you Antionette," he went on, "are the spitting image of your mother."

He deliberately gave Rachelle a smirk. If her children were not with her, he would probably have jumped her bones right there. His lust for her was over-powering. She turned him on, each time resisting his attention. The fire in her was more than he could control. But he really wanted her, and badly. Cedric only wanted to show her that, he could be her *love-master*.

He pictured her begging for more. There was a lot more he intended to give the woman who was like a goddess to him.

When I finish with her, my name and image will be embedded in her brain for sure. He thought.

"Why thank you," Antionette smiled, "many others have said the same thing after meeting Mom."

Rachelle was still at a loss for words. Cedric's sudden appearance had thrown her off guard. She felt that if she did not say something and quickly; her son and daughter might really draw the wrong conclusion, about her relationship with the shifty stranger.

"Amazing memory," Rachelle finally remarked, "to retain so much about us."

She wanted him to stop undressing her. Anthony and Antionette were becoming suspicious. Rachelle could tell by the way that they watched her expressions whenever Cedric spoke; they also noticed him as well.

"Oh, so you know one another," Anthony was quick to ask. Then he directed an inquisitive look at his Mom.

Something was not right. And her son could not put his finger on it. The guy appeared to be hot for his mother. He knew she was sharp, and had often wondered why she had never remarried, or even chose to date ever since his father left.

"Not really," Rachelle was too fast for comfort, "Cedric is the band leader at the Deuces club where Lori, Lisa, and I go once in awhile."

She looked at Cedric and hoped that he read her expression to back off. He had no right appearing out of now-where ruining her peace. He was becoming a second shadow. Why in hell was he following her, like a animal in heat? Lately it seemed as though he owned every business she frequented.

He cannot be hard-up for me, she thought. *I've seen many different women in his company.*

"Well it was nice talking with you," he was pleasant, but phony. "Please enjoy your meal, and feel free to stop in anytime."

He had given them an open invitation, but Rachelle had no intension of obliging his offer. *The nerve* she thought.

"That was odd," Antionette remarked, "he spoke as if he knew us."

"It was, wasn't it," Rachelle sighed, "sometime people do things to impress others. He's probably narcissistic."

They laughed at that remark. But Rachelle was pissed off. She had done her best to stay cool, and not give Cedric the satisfaction of knowing that he was getting under her skin.

They finished their meal and left. Each was thankful that they had one another.

After the restaurant incident, Rachelle found herself again looking over her shoulder where ever she went. It was not that she had PPD (Paranoid Personality Disorder). She just did not trust Cedric.

Even though he was a known killer, she did not feel threatened by him. But she also felt that he would do whatever was necessary to conceal his illegal activities. How *else would he not have served a day behind bars?* Then Cedric was a professional, when it came to covering his tracks.

Lori and Lisa wanted her to move in with them for awhile. They feared for her safety; home alone. Naturally she appreciated their concern, but she was not going to let Cedric or anyone else force her out of her place.

Soon thereafter, Rachelle and the girls planned a long weekend getaway to Nassau. Packed and ready for some real fun and plenty of relaxation on the beaches of the Bahamas Islands; Rachelle was anxiously awaiting her ride.

I must be his first stop. She thought. Usually other passengers were picked-up on the way to the airport. That was not a problem; she was really ready for an escape from her current stressful environment. Some beauty rest and solace was just what the doctor would have ordered.

Rachelle texted the girls, letting them know that she was on her way. She did not realize that the shuttle driver had headed away from their destination.

"Excuse me sir," she inquired, "this is not the way to the airport."

Maybe there was no need for concern. There was more than one particular way that he could go. She just did not want to miss her flight.

"Sorry Miss," the driver informed, "but there's a reported accident ahead of us. I had to detour. I also have one pick-up that is close to your drop-off."

After speaking on his cell phone; the man at the wheel then directed his attention to the traffic. Rachelle looked at her watch calculating their arrival. She had plenty of time before check-in.

They made the one stop that the driver had mentioned. But before she could get a good look at where they were, someone pulled her from the van. Two strange looking men carried her towards a car; parked behind what appeared to be a vacant building.

Rachelle fought to get away, screaming for help. But no one came to her rescue. The oversize men over-powered her. They put her in the vehicle; then tied her feet and hands. One of them also covered her eyes, with a handkerchief over her nose.

Whatever it was made her dizzy; she quickly passed out. The fearful woman, had been kidnapped, drugged, and carried off; someplace other than the airport where her friends were waiting.

Rachelle awoke incapacitated; hand-cuffed to a king-sized bed, having no idea about her whereabouts. The blindfold had been removed. She looked around only to find that she was in a very dim empty room with barred windows.

Where are my clothes? She wondered.

Rachelle had been dressed in red satin gown, and bare backed heels that matched. What about her clothes? Who would do this?

She yelled for help, but each time, it was as if her voice ricocheted back to her. The helpless female's cries were all for nothing, the room was hollow. Her hapless voice was merely an echo to her ears. Unable to move, she found herself in a predicament that brought back unwelcomed memories.

How long had she been here? She really did not know. There was no way she could tell whether it was day or night. The windows looked dark and had been covered with black paint.

Her elevated heart beat ticked like a time bomb. It also reminded her of an empty barrel that someone might beat over and over again. She felt as though she was might be nearing a heart attack.

Was she here to be tortured, killed or what? If so, then why? To her clear knowledge, she had not caused anyone any trouble. Frightened and at a loss for answers, Rachelle found herself detained, hungry, thirsty, and desperately wanting to go home. Whatever the case, she had hoped that her family and friends would be looking for her—and very soon.

Then, she heard footsteps outside the room. A masked man entered. He freed one hand from the handcuffs and untied her feet. Then he placed a tray with food and water on the bed.

"Who are you?" She was really scared. "Why am I here?"

The mysterious figure did not answer. He only stood against the near wall waiting to observe her eating and drinking.

Something is better than nothing, Rachelle thought. She ate some of the soup and took a few sips of water. She pushed the tray away immediately, wishing that both hands were free. There was no defending herself like this. The liquid had a peculiarly funny taste. Was she being drugged again?

The guard removed the tray directly, and proceeded to re-secure her free hand to the bed post.

"I don't know who are or my reason for being here," she was nervous, "but you won't get away with this."

Rachelle wanted to appear strong to her captives.

He stood looking at her through the round holes in the mask. He remained silent. He locked the door behind him; and disappeared.

She later heard a voice surrounding the room. She looked about, noticing speakers in each corner of the wall; and a device appearing to be a mounted camera.

"If you do as you are told," she was instructed, "no one will harm you."

There was no reason why she would make herself weaker than she actually was; by trying to shake loose. For now, she was in restraints and a prisoner to someone who refused to reveal their identity.

"Why are you doing this to me?" Rachelle pleaded, "Where am I?"

There was a long silence before she heard anything.

"Be quiet," he was cold, "You are here to please me. If you don't, your family will suffer dearly the consequences of your not cooperating."

Then fear gripped her heart and would not let go. The pain was unbearable. She called out for help. She felt as if her life was in very serious jeopardy.

"My family and the police are looking for me," she trembled, "they will find me."

Rachelle had never felt fear like this. Tears streamed down her face. There was no fight in her. Weak and lost, she laid there waiting for it all to end. She was drowsy from the drugs he had continuously given her.

Again, she found herself still in bondage, donning a black shear gown and matching slippers.

Who could the crazy person be, and why was he dressing her in such provocative sleepwear? What else had he done to her?

The room keeper disguised his voice, making it most difficult to recognize. He had made it clear that if she did not do as he asked, her children's safety would be at risk.

Now she had to pull her thoughts together and if possible, find a way out of this dark place.

She was a survivor and had hoped that if she gave in to him, perhaps he would let down his guard.

"What is it that you want from me," she repeated again and again.

Rachelle heard the door open and footsteps nearing the bed; she was close to hyperventilating, but did her best to remain calm.

"Be still," he commanded, "remember, do what I say"

With that he began rubbing her breasts, licking and kissing her pointed nipples. The kidnapper whispered in her ear things that he intended to do to her.

His soft and hot lips lapped her ears. The confused woman dared not resist whatever he did. Her family's lives had already been threatened by him.

He continued lusting over her tensed body. At one point he opened her legs with both hands, gliding up and down each thigh— paying close attention to the most inner parts.

N. O.

Although she did not want to react, the touch of his tongue on the lower part of her stomach, ignited warmth throughout her body. She was forced to feel excitement. The way in which he treated her body caused the heated female to have flashbacks of the hall encounter with Cedric. And although he sounded cold, he was gentle with her.

Then she felt the weight of his body on hers. The way his sexual organ felt against her, was similar to the manner in which the band leader had pushed himself close to her that time at Deuces.

Could this be a coincidence? How was it that one and one added up?

If it was you-know-who, then Rachelle would probably have to think very quickly on her back.

"You don't have to keep me handcuffed or tied-up," she said. "I'll do whatever you want to keep my children safe."

She feared that he was so aroused, that her longing to be released in order to please him would not matter. He Ignored her plea; rubbing his body atop hers.

Then, he entered, having his way with her. No boundaries were barred. He was having it against her will. Whatever he was doing felt too good. But why could it not have been the right man instead of this guy?

All his moves caused her body to react without permission. And although he was surely sick in the worse way, still she wanted to touch him. His breathing increased as he reached climax.

Rachelle had hoped that he would leave her. After all, he had gotten what he wanted. But instead he just laid there, his manhood thumping inside her. He cupped and kissed her breasts again.

"You do things to me," he spoke softly. "I don't want anyone to have you but me."

She had heard the exact same words before. Her mind was clouded with satisfying thoughts of pleasure.

"Remove the cuffs," Rachelle tried to persuade, "I can't make love to you like this."

She hoped that he would listen this time.

"Later," he replied.

Then he left her again. What was it about her; that attracted men like this? First it was No Name who wanted her to spank and dress him like a woman. Now there was this pervert who had kidnapped and had his way with her.

Rachelle was really pissed. No one threatens to do harm to her family and get away with it. For now she would be his sex slave. But once she was able to convince him to unchain her; the tables would no doubt turn, she vowed.

During his next visit, she revealed that she knew who he was. Her tormentor was Cedric. She could not believe that he would stoop so low. The only way that he could have her, was against her will.

"Rachelle," he started, "I didn't want it to be this way. I've wanted you since that night at Deuces."

Cedric sounded sympathetic. But she could not believe this. More than likely it was a trick. How could she give in to him after what he had put her through? And she really knew without a doubt, that he would kill her family and maybe even her friends, if she did not do what he wanted.

He went on to tell her that he had never felt this desperate for any woman. And that she had awakened something in him that had been buried since the birth of his son. His wife had left subsequent to that.

The captured woman really did not give a damn about his sob story. And felt that he had gotten what he deserved. Good for him that his wife and son had left his ass. That was, if it had really happened. Cedric was not one to be trusted.

"But, why do this," she questioned.

"I might have come around eventually," she lied.

Now was the time to put her plan into action.

"Take these off," Rachelle stretched out her hands. "I can't go anywhere in this cage." The holding room was like that to her.

He looked at her, as if he was searching for an answer from himself, whether he could trust her or not. Then he slowly removed the handcuffs, and united her feet.

Cedric took her hands in his, and helped her off the bed. He embraced Rachelle like a man hungry for compassion.

With his right hand, he lifted hers overhead; then encircled her waist with the left arm. He backed her against the wall, beginning to sex her. This went on awhile before he led her from the room to another. They were both nude. Was he taking her to another chamber of fright?

Rachelle was relieved to see that it was a bathroom with a shower. She wanted to wash him from her body.

Rachelle's commander, with soap in hand, began to rub and lather her body from head to toe. Cedric turned her face toward the shower wall, where he gently washed her—moving slowly down each leg and up again.

She welcomed the feel of warm water, but then wished that he would stop. She could bath herself. But she did not want to upset him. This was probably a test by him to assure that she understood his demands.

Then her plan was to play along until the right opportunity presented itself. In the meantime, things that he did to her were really exciting. Had he been aware that it felt that good to her, he would maintain more control. Nonetheless, she was turned on by the feeling of his warmness.

Cedric was the master of his skills. It was obvious, that it did not bother him if he had to take a person out—or have them disappear.

He turned her around to face him, looking as if he could see through her. With his body close to hers, he made love in a way that she had not quite experienced before.

I could fall for this. Please stop, I can't take anymore.

She found herself grasping him tightly, but then moaning against her will. She begged him to stop. But he continued his quest to have her submit to his steamy desire.

Afterward, he washed her again and rinsed the soapy bubbles from her body. He slowly dried her, taking time to gloat at the slim, smooth, and seductive image.

Then he escorted her to yet another room. It was much nicer than the last. The sleep area was surrounded with an ensemble of night stands, king size bed, carpeted floor, and more windows with bars. However there was no television or telephone in sight.

A table by the window was decorated with flowers and fresh fruit. He promised to bring her food and water later, then left, locking the door. This time he did not put her in handcuffs or tie her like an animal.

She quickly put her ear against the door listening to his footsteps heading down the hall. Then she went to look out the windows noticing only nearby woods. There was nothing else in sight. She was hidden in the wilderness of this place. But at least she would be able to count the days going by. Right now, she could only see light—and night would come too soon.

Later, he returned carrying a tray with something for her to eat as he had promised. Cedric sat it on a table, his head hung low.

In the midst of it all, he confessed his love for her—asking for forgiveness.

Did he take her for a fool or what? Rachelle knew that he could never let her go.

She felt that only one of them would leave this place alive, and the determined woman, would do everything in her power to be that person.

"How long have I been here," she asked softly.

She really hoped that Lori and Lisa had notified the police that she was missing.

"What does it matter?" he replied, "no one is looking for you."

What had he done? It surely was not the answer Rachelle wanted to hear. By now her children and everyone else would be concerned. It was certainly out-of- the-norm for her to go off without letting them know her whereabouts.

"What do you mean?" She quizzed.

"I've taken care of everything," he responded.

His look was blank and seemed emotionless.

Now she had really lost her appetite. Had he already eliminated her children, Lori and Lisa? This was now the straw that broke the camel's back—and he had to go for sure.

Many days and nights had past, and he continued to have his way with her. Although he was not mean or rough, he forced her to do things; that was slowly causing the old Rachelle to emerge. She could not wait to make him pay dearly.

Rachelle prayed that her family was still safe. She could not get it out of her mind, the picture of him doing to them what he had done at the beach. She figured that because he was such a thug, that Cedric probably did not go anywhere without a fire arm on his person.

But how could she check? He was nude each time, physically invading her body. He would parade before her as if he was more than proud of his manhood. The woman-taker sensed that Rachelle watched his well-built body; so he wanted to turn her on. Her mind raced as if she was on a speed track.

He had to clothe himself sooner or later, she knew. That was when she would probably get a chance to overtake him, she had hoped. Then her prayers would be answered. Her guess was that a week had passed since the kidnapping.

She sat by the window in a short purple gown he had previously put at the foot of the bed; when she heard the key turn in the door. He stood there in a grey pin stripped designer suit; as if seeking approval in the choice of his attire.

Now, do your stuff girl. This may be your one and only chance. She thought.

"My, don't you look fine," her compliment was false, "are you stepping out?"

He had a garment bag in his hand. Was he really going to let her go free? This was not easy to think about. She still believed that his plan was to use and eliminate all evidence—including Rachelle.

"No, I thought some clothes would make you feel better," he was calm.

But she was not falling for that. He probably did not want anyone to see him leave his house with something that might look suspicious. But if he was seen leaving the house with a well-dressed female, then no one might pay that much attention to it.

"I think that would be great," she tried to sound convincing.

Rachelle stood by the chair, letting the night gown slowly slide down her body to the floor. She took time walking toward Cedric who could not take his eyes off the firm boobs. The sexual woman removed his jacket, slowly placing it close beside the bed. Then she unbuttoned his shirt, and unbuckled the wanting man's belt.

She looked at him with a false desire as his pants lowered to the floor. Rubbing herself against his hardness, she knelt to remove his shoes, one at a time. She looked up as if he was her master.

Then, Rachelle pulled him to the floor, like a very skilled female; straddling his body, kissing his ears, face, and chest. She worked her body from side to side, up and down. Inching her way down each thigh; she kissed and rubbed his body all over.

Then she reached between his legs and held onto his manhood. The moaning confirmed that she now had him in the palms of her desperate hands.

"What do you want," she teased in a whisper, "I really want to please you."

Her time had finally come. He would soon be at her mercy, she somehow thought.

"Close your eyes," she instructed intimately, "and open your mouth."

That killer characteristic that she had locked away for so long was out—and it wanted revenge. Now she had to do what it took to survive. It was him—or her. It felt good hearing him beg and call her name out loud.

She placed a breast in his mouth, feeling him suckle as an infant would a bottle. Then Rachelle moved his hands to her buttocks, and commanded him to grasp each cheek.

While he was in the heat of that, she sneaked a search of his coat, perhaps hoping there was a weapon inside the pocket. But she found nothing.

The know-what-to-do-woman turned him over face-down. Then she massaged his round, solid rear; and with one hand she fumbled his pants. Then her fingers touched what felt like a firearm.

Rachelle's suspicion had it! Yet, she did not want to deprive him of one last orgasm. At the same time, he wanted her to experience the pleasure of being with him.

Rachelle turned him over, kissing all of him except his lips. Hers was not to be a goodbye smooch, but the last call for life.

"I will always love you Rachelle," he confessed. "You have made me whole."

With her right hand to her side, she quickly pushed backward, standing with the gun pointed at the front of his torso.

"Rachelle," he yelled, "what are you doing?"

Backing away to put distance between them; she looked at him with an expression that could take out a military unit.

"I'm saving my family," she declared through clenched teeth, "and myself from you. You threatened my children."

She also wanted him to know that forcing her to submit made her feel indecent. The look of fear on his face was the same as what she and the girls had; the night when they witnessed him, take someone's life.

"Rachelle," he was frightened, "it was all a plot to have you to myself. I could never harm you or your children."

She squint her eyes in disgust. It was as if she could look through him, but saw nothing except anger. Time was wasting. She needed to get this over with.

"Yes you would," she shouted, "you wouldn't waste a minute on mercy for me or anyone else. I saw you kill that guy at the beach."

He stared at her, giving the impression that he would surely kill her now. She had seen something that no one else knew about. And he could not afford to let her breathe a word of it. He waited desperately for a chance to take the gun.

The controlled victim realized that she had just said too much. Now he had to make a move to take her out—or else.

Rachelle shot one, two, three, four times, then once or twice more... unloading the pistol. She wanted to be sure that he would never breathe again.

In the aftermath, she had done the community a favor. Cedric would never get the chance to put someone else through what she had just experienced. She was sure that he had done this before and gotten away with it.

Rachelle recalled seeing a telephone in the hallway and very calmly went for it. Then decided that it was best to use the cell phone; the house phone was not such a very good idea. Police would more than likely check it for all calls made. So, after a moment of contemplation, she used Cedric's mobile phone. Then she would dispose of it directly once it had served its purpose.

Why was she not nervous? The "B" Rachelle was not one to lose her cool.

She was calm enough to call Lori.

"Hello," she spoke clearly, "It's me. I'll explain later, but for now I want you to call Lisa. I need you guys to come and get me."

Then she questioned herself. *How can they rescue me?* Rachelle had no idea where she was. Asking Lori to hold on, she searched Cedric's jacket for anything that would give her a clue on her whereabouts.

Then she searched the place hoping to find postal delivery of mail, or anything with an address listed. In the hallway on an end table were a stack of magazines. They were addressed to Mr. Cedric Elderrey. Rachelle hurried to give Lori the information. She had to take a calculated guess, that it was her location.

She found her luggage under the bed, and changed into shorts and a simple white top.

There was time to wipe away anything that would indicate her presence in the house. *Better safe than sorry*, she thought.

As she attempted to clear anything that might later incriminate her; Rachelle came across something that looked very familiar. It was a silver attaché case like the one Cedric had the night that they followed him.

She opened the case slowly—finding it full of money. It did not appear to be such a big deal; for back in the day, she had seen much more cash.

She planned to take it with her. After-all she had earned it. And if things did not pan out as she might hope; there may be a need for it. Then a top notch attorney would cost a lot.

She decided not to move the body. Someone might find it before long.

Rachelle kept a watchful eye for the girls. Soon, a vehicle pulled up that looked like Lori's. After she checked to be certain that it was the girls; she left what had been her torture chamber, for far too long. With the case in hand, she quickly got in the rear seat, not looking back.

Lori and Lisa were overjoyed to see their buddy. Afterwards, the ride home was silent. Each engrossed in their own summation of; what took place while Rachelle was missing. There would be time to talk later. But, for now they were glad that she was safe.

ACE IN THE HOLE

It was a good feeling being home; back comfortably in her environment and safe from a nymphomaniac. After taking a long hot shower, Rachelle crawled into bed. Sleep took over immediately.

Rachelle woke late from what was a well-needed rest. The brave mother, who did what had to be done to keep her children safe, had not thought once about the decision to take Cedric out. She had found the nerve and strength to remove him without remorse.

Although it was one in the afternoon, it was breakfast for her. She had gone too long without the option of a highly loaded meal. Today she would pull no punches with food. The cholesterol filled meal was not what the doctor might have recommended, but served the purpose.

So be it. Life was too short for the minor stuff. After eating, she called her buddies, but no one answered. She headed back to her room, changing into sweats for comfort.

Soon after, she heard the doorbell ring. Rachelle thought that it was Lori and Lisa, and hurried to answer. The two leaning on the door fell inside when it opened.

"Look, why did you take so long," Lori was out of breath. "That damn heat really takes my energy."

Rachelle was amused by her panting. They had no idea how happy she was to be with them again. So much had happened.

"We didn't want to wait," Lisa spoke, "for you to call us. So, here we are."

They embraced one another holding on as if it would be their last. Well, that might have been the case had it not been for Rachelle's quick thinking.

They took seats in the living room, still on edge, and waited for Rachelle to say something. They desperately wanted to air their concern, especially since she did not meet them at the airport.

Lori did her best to be patient. But how could she be if it were any longer. Her head was still in a whirl from the numerous calls she and

Lisa made, attempting to reach her. It was also not like her to be late. When it came to going on trips, Rachelle was mostly the early bird.

After there was no answer from all the calls, they had no choice but to contact Anthony, Jr. and Antionette. Kirk and Jerome were also informed. The girls thought maybe they could be of some help.

"Girl," Lori stressed, "I was so afraid that something terrible had happened."

She was teary and could barely speak. The emotional friend was hysterical at one point, at the thought that harm had come to her buddy. Rachelle was touched by her friend's outpouring.

"Actually," Lisa spoke softly, "My first thought was that it had to involve that creepy Cedric. I would never put anything past him after what we saw at the beach."

It had been awhile since the incident, but it was as though it was yesterday for the girls. At that time, everyone was on pins and needles each time that the telephone or doorbell rang. Lori and Lisa had gotten to the point where something as simple, as answering the door or phone kept them on edge.

"I can't tell you the sadness that surrounded Lisa and I," Lori went on, "it was pure torture not knowing if we would ever see you again."

They sat quietly, each thankful to be alive and safe. The three had been together through thick and thin, ups and downs.

They had faced the good, bad, and worse, yet had always maintained a strong and committed friendship.

A while later, Rachelle confirmed, that their fears of Cedric's involvement with her missing in action; were not just assumptions, nor their reaching into mid-air for conclusions, but that it was a fact.

She watched their expressions closely as they looked at each other in silence. Rachelle felt that they wanted to know all the details, but decided that if all was told; her friends may not be able to handle it.

However, she would very carefully reveal only the basics about the devastating kidnapping. *Why involve them?* What if her decisions came back to haunt her?

"Well," she started, "I will say that I was really afraid. I didn't know what was going on until it was too late."

Rachelle had been pushed into a situation where survival was priority. And the safety of her family came before anything or anyone else. Although her past was not something she wanted to remember; in an odd way she welcomed the experience. Back then, it had kept her alive and many times.

"Before I could react," she continued, "someone was pulling me out of the van, and drugging me with something, I don't know what."

Lori and Lisa sat there shaking as if it had happened to them. And to think, they thought their fear was worse. But Rachelle's appeared to be much more as they listened.

"I awoke to find myself," she paused, "handcuffed and tied to a bed."

Now, their faces were consumed with frowns, their mouths were opened wide as her buddies gasped in horror.

"When did you know that it was him," Lisa asked.

What was she to say now? Rachelle had never shared with them how Cedric had pushed himself on her in the hallway, next to the lady's room at Deuces that time.

"I remember some of the things," she went on, "he had said to me in the club and beside his car that night."

Killing Cedric did not bother her at all. It was just another do or die circumstance, that she had to handle. Now, she was ready for whatever may follow. And she would eliminate anything, or anyone that might be detrimental, to her and love ones.

So, Sora Nora Cedric, she thought.

Then, she looked away briefly to shield the tears that were beginning to flood her eyes. Rachelle was really emotional, yet and still balanced. Her friends could never imagine what she had been through; neither did she have any clue about their ordeal during the separation.

"How in the world did you get free," Lisa really wanted to know.

"I was lucky," she answered, "I convinced him to unchain me."

There was no way she could find the words to tell them the whole truth. It was over and she wanted to move on. Enough with the questions; she wanted to put it all behind her. But she felt that she owed them perhaps a little more than what had been given.

"I think that I've heard more than expected," Lori understood. "We don't want to wear her out with all the questions. The important fact is that she is here now. We will deal with the rest at another time."

"Thanks so much," Rachelle appreciated, "for caring guys. But I would like to know if you called the police."

She had to know more about what the girls had done when they realized that something was wrong.

"No we didn't do that," Lori responded very quickly," your son thought it best we hold off on contacting authorities. He wanted to check out a few things first."

"That's good," Rachelle was relieved, "you took Anthony's advice. No need having the police questioning everyone. I'm sure that you guys were in no shape for that."

So, she would call her children later. They needed to know that she was just fine. As for Lori and Lisa, Rachelle strongly felt that the less they knew the better things would probably be. As usual, she was their dedicated protector.

"So, how about a toast for good health and good friends," she suggested, "I have some finger food in the dining room, and your favorite Mascota."

She had removed a few items from Cedric's *love* hut. It was her insurance in case things did not turn out as she had hoped. They were locked away safely; just in case she might need them.

Time was not waiting for her or anyone else. Whatever was done; was just that. Then there was no breaking away from the sure and strong hands of fate.

She had covered her tracks well, and protected herself from any possible repercussion. For in her possession were the tapes which Cedric had filmed and recorded; when he held Rachelle prisoner against her will.

ONE TOO MANY

Life has a funny way of getting attention. So much had happened, by bringing the three of them to the stairway of hope and happiness.

Sometime after Rachelle's kidnapping, Lori and Kirk had planned to marry. The two lovebirds wanted their ceremony to be special and unforgettable. So they decided to have their wedding on one of the lovely beaches of Jamaica.

To Rachelle's surprise, she was asked to be Lori's maid of honor. At first Lisa was really hurt. She just knew that it would be her. After all, she was Lori's friend before Rachelle even moved to California.

After much apology and convincing, Lisa began to come around. Lori did not want her to get stressed out with the duties of being the matron. Rachelle usually kept a calm persona, and could probably handle the last minute decisions, that at times take place in situations such as wedding planning.

Lori and Kirk's wedding was an all white affair. All the guests wore that designated color. That included the table decorations and the hired band for entertainment as well.

And although it was Kirk and Lori's time, the three buddies had finally gotten their island getaway together.

Rachelle, Lisa, and Jerome returned home after a week of partying, touring the beautiful island, and stuffing themselves with food and drinks.

Lori and Kirk stayed on a week longer; after all, they needed to enjoy their honeymoon without having buddies along.

It was really odd, Lori not leaving with them. They had never been apart since their first meeting. They had been friends just that long.

It took the men awhile to separate them after their goodbyes at the airport.

They thought it amusing watching the women boo-who. But for Rachelle, Lori, and Lisa, it was as if a part of themselves was being snatched away. Then that is what friends are about. To laugh and cry together, enjoy the happy and not so happy times together, and most of all, stick together.

These true and loyal friends had bonded early on. Their lasting friendship had looked forward to aging together. They had even talked about calling themselves *Seniors on the Move*.

The plane ride home for *two* was a sad one. They not only talked themselves to sleep, but poor Jerome as well. He was no match for their detailed reminiscing.

Then it was back to the old grind, that they called work. Rachelle focused on another project and spent a lot of time with new clients. She put in quite a bit of overtime. Some evenings after working twelve and sometimes fifteen hours, she only had enough energy to shower and call it a night.

Two weeks of that routine was really wearing her down. Rachelle found herself working at home more than usual, just to get away from the office. One more day and she would have time off from the hassle of it all. She had not taken any vacation since returning from Jamaica. Friday could not come soon enough for her. The girl was beat and really needed some R&R (Rest and Rehabilitation).

Then Lori and Kirk returned from their honeymoon. It was time to hang out, and chat, about married life, expectations, and whatever else.

Rachelle woke early Friday, ready to start her day and get it over with. Stopping only to activate her security alarm, she hurried out the door.

"Got darn it," she yelled, "what the hell!"

She had almost cussed tripping over a box on the front steps.

"This again," she questioned, "give me a break."

She was very upset, rubbing her right foot. That was one reason she disliked wearing sandals; either she would hit against something or someone would step on her feet. The problem with her shoes was that too many toes were exposed.

After a moment of examining herself for any bruises; she looked down to see that the attacker was a red box wrapped with a large black bow. Then she looked around to see if anyone nearby watched as she closely checked the box.

The card attached was addressed to Mrs. Rachelle WynHurst-Meyers. Now her heart rate really began to increase, for sure. Who was it this time, playing games? She decided not to open the box, because she knew without a doubt, the content.

But no one other than family and friends knew that she was married. Yet, the sender had noted her whole name in its entirety.

She quickly removed the neat package, taking it to the car. Rachelle took a moment to clear her head. She remembered the call she had gotten from the girls not long ago.

"Girl," Lori reported, "our worries are over. Did you hear about Cedric?"

She appeared in a hurry to give her friend some good news about something she had just heard.

"No," Rachelle replied. "What is it?"

She had a feeling what it was that her friend wanted to share with her. Anyway, she would listen with a keen ear.

"Rachelle," Lori went on, "They found him all shot up, dead, but they did not say where."

It was surely a relief to hear that the location was not revealed, by whomever or wherever this news came from.

"That's right," Lisa burst in. "The word is that police don't have a clue at this time just who wasted Cedric."

She had no idea that they were on a three-way. The girls seemed too happy about a loss of life; even if they had not cared about, nor trusted Cedric. Then his fate was simply something they had just heard about.

Rachelle was well aware how information could get twisted, and blown out of proportion. Then there were times when her friends would, get caught up in the moment of that kind of stuff.

"Well then," Lisa went on, "it's buzzing all around town that he had finally met his maker."

These women were back and forth with the good news. Rachelle had to alternate the telephone from one ear to the other. That was how long this fresh, hot chatter was.

"Yeah," Lori reported, "Kirk said a buddy of his heard that whoever did it; shot him numerous times; and left his naked body on the floor of one of his out of the way houses."

She really did not need to be filled in about all of this. If truth be told, she could give them the real deal; but she had kept that part from them both.

"Look," Rachelle said, "I've been pulling some really long hours at work since Jamaica, and this is my first to hear anything."

"Well," Lisa responded, "it is circulating that his funeral services were put on hold, until the next of kin was located."

Rachelle was glad to hear from them, but she really did not want her ears worn out listening to the gossip, that her friends were sharing.

Now her mind raced to find answers as to who might have sent her flowers once again.

What sort of game was it? It surely was not Cedric. He was dead now.

This time she would not freak out. Rachelle did not want to go back inside, so she took the strange delivery to work.

Maybe it wasn't Cedric who sent the roses the first time, she questioned herself. Before she had waited until the last minute until she told Lori and Lisa about the mysterious package. But, she would not hesitate this time.

Later, arriving at work, her first telephone call was to the girls.

"Good morning Mrs. Bevins," Rachelle greeted, "how are you?"

There were times when she joked with Lori; it was like watching a favorite comedy show. Her friend thought that her married name was something bland. However, Rachelle thought that it had a very nice ring to the ear.

"I'm fine," Lori replied, "I see you have jokes so early in the morning."

Rachelle could not stop laughing. She knew that she was about to set Lori off. The girl did not like to be left dangling when it came to receiving information. She was a say-it-quick, and move on with it person. Her buddy, the jokester, was just attempting to warm her friend up for what was about to come.

"I almost broke my ankle leaving the house," Rachelle admitted.

She did not know how Lori would react, once she heard what had happened.

"How so," her girl laughed, "have you been drinking already?"

"Of course not," Rachelle said. "I tripped over a box on the front steps and hit my toes. I didn't see the damn thing until it was too late."

"Yep," sounds to me like you had a few before work," Lori amused.

Then Rachelle felt that Kirk was rubbing off on her. Now she would have to deal with two unpaid comedians.

"Certainly not," Rachelle responded. "I was rushing out after setting the alarm. You know that thing acts funny at times. Then, before I knew it, my poor toes were burning from hitting against the box."

There was no response from Lori. It appeared that she was listening to everything her buddy had to say.

"I looked down after massaging my toes; to see a beautiful long red box, wrapped with a silk ribbon. And the card was addressed to me."

"What did you do with the box," Lori asked.

She could just picture her sweating on the end of her nose. Rachelle was taking too long to give her all the details.

"Well," Rachelle continued, "I brought it to work and put them in my office."

The friend on the other end did not readily reply. It was dead air between the two.

"Are you kidding me," Lori answered finally. "Tell me this isn't starting again."

Lori did not feel that it was such a good idea to take the flowers to work. But then, what was Rachelle supposed to do, leave them home? At least on the job, she could give them to her secretary. That would work for now.

"Suppose we were wrong the first time," Rachelle went on, "about the sender being Cedric? He's gone, so who could it be this time?"

Both agreed that it was probably a mistake. They might have been a little too hasty. So who was the suspect now?

Then Rachelle felt that it was not a good idea to tell her hyper friend. She was not as reserved as Lisa. It was as if she could hear Lori's volcano of an attitude starting to erupt.

"Well, like I suggested," Lori seemed furious, "give them away, send them to a nursing home, do anything, just don't keep the darn flowers."

The heated buddy's temper was not letting up. Her day had really changed for the worse; thanks to some fool, who had to be hot for her roll-partner.

"Look," Rachelle proposed, "we'll discuss it later. I'd like for you to call Lisa, and let her know. I'll be on conference calls, and in meetings most of the day."

Rachelle was not trying to do a double-jeopardy with another call. Lori would be her liaison.

"No problem," Lori assured, I got you girl. I just hope that we don't have to live the flower nightmare again. We were all a ball of nerves the last time."

Then she wondered how Lisa would take the news. Although Rachelle felt that she sometimes handled things a little calmer, Lori had seen her buddy go off the edge a few times. Would this be one of those moments? She would surely see.

"Thanks girl," Rachelle was relieved, "I'll call you later."

YESTERDAY IS GONE

That day at work Rachelle stayed until around four. She handled everything that required her attention.

She was really looking forward to a night out with her friends. She wanted to relieve the stress of work.

This time of day, she would usually beat the evening traffic getting home. It seemed as if everybody drove to work on Fridays. Well, she had news for them. She was home in no time.

It really felt good not having to work for the next couple of weeks. She poured a glass of her favorite wine, and headed for the shower.

Rachelle had planned to take a nap before the guys pick her up. After bathing, the now fresh and relaxed woman, laid across the bed, and listened to the new R&B CD she purchased a month ago. Just before dozing off, the telephone rang.

"Hello," she answered.

There it was again, no answer, only the piercing of the dial tone.

OK, I'm going to just let it play itself out this time. It's probably a wrong number. She told herself.

She hung up, turned up the music, finishing her drink.

Soon after, the doorbell rang. Rachelle reached for the white shorts and top she had laid out before showering. It was still daylight, and some neighbors cut their grass and washed their cars.

She opened the door and felt her legs give away. For, there in the flesh was her husband, Anthony Sr. He immediately dropped the gift box from hand reaching to catch his wife. She had fainted.

With his assistance, she was able to make it across the room to a chair. Rachelle was shocked and in disbelief, that the ghost of the man she deeply loved, and had not seen in years, was now in her presence again.

Weakened, and barely able to speak, Rachelle asked for a glass of water. Was she dreaming? Or was it a mirage? Her feelings were mixed now. Anthony had been gone for more than twenty years. And now he shows his face, giving her nerves a jump start that she had never anticipated.

But if she did not love him so much, there would be no problem adding him to her list of corpses.

Anthony had a lot of explaining to do, about why he stayed away from his family for so long. Rachelle had decided that if he did not appear to be genuine, she would give him a gigantic boot in the rear— out of her sight. After all, he had already been missing from her life for far too long.

Then what kind of fool was she, to continue holding on to empty hope? Could it be that her wedding vows were, as important to her, as the air she breathed?

Soon Anthony returned with the water, in a shaking hand, passing it to Rachelle.

To him, she was still as lovely as the day he had left. How would he begin telling her the reason he had to leave his family—never to show his face again?

After taking a few sips of water, Rachelle sat the glass on a nearby table. The pain that Anthony had experienced for more than a score; was nothing compared to what he felt now, watching his wife feel it also.

He reached out to comfort her, but she pulled away. Could he blame her for wanting him to keep his distance? Anthony nearly froze, taking a seat on the sofa facing Rachelle.

"Sweetheart," he began, "I know that my being here after such a long time is really a shock for you."

Rachelle did not speak. She simply watched him as one would a stranger desiring to be heard. That is all he wanted.

"There were many times that I wanted to reach out to you and the children," he went on. "But it was not safe. Your lives depended on my doing what was instructed."

She observed how he struggled to find the right words.

All the time that he was away from us, it should be easy now, to just come right out with it. Just tell me, damn it. She thought.

"What do you mean," she asked, "not safe."

She just wanted the truth, and nothing more. There were so many questions that needed answers. Her brain filled with just that.

What would the children do or say once they knew that their missing father had returned? Although he was alive, would he then be dead to them?

Although they had never heard her say one negative thing about him; there were many times she had cussed him out to herself. Times were rough back then. There she was, a young mother, left to fend for self and her offspring.

Then would Rachelle find it in heart to forgive him for the numerous times she had to struggle in order to make ends meet? Not to mention, some really bad things she did to keep things going. The decisions she made, taking her to those places that still caused her to cringe, even today.

Having been turned out by a man she trusted as a friend, Rachelle had found herself in the escort business. In her new profession, the money was a very good draw for those things needed to raise a family. However, that line of work was very risky and by no means, safe.

Because she was independent, a few pimps were determined to bring her in under their rigid rule of thumb. But Rachelle continued to turn down the offers.

Then sometime later, she was attacked on the way home by one of those predatory free-loaders. And in an attempt to defend herself, Rachelle cut the man's throat with a broken bottle she picked up from the ground, causing his untimely demise.

Thereafter, she became an advocate for women who were abused and forced into prostitution. Rachelle wanted to help ladies of the night, young girls, and runaways; afraid and fearing for their lives—trying to leave the street life.

Because of her support for those women, Rachelle had some run-ins with street pimps threatening her. But they paid the price later—she eliminated them.

What type of life did women have by selling themselves to fill the pockets of a pimp? Someone who would never free them, rather keep them on the sex-for-sale list.

So be it for her, if a few pimps were no longer allowed to breathe.

"If you recalled," Anthony continued, "my dad was never around, only my mother."

That was true. She had never seen his father. And she often wondered why that was. But Rachelle knew that Anthony's mother was a jewel. Then her passing had taken a toll on him. That much she understood about it.

"I remember," she urged him, "what else?"

She was not going to be soft and mushy, if he was trying to hand her a sob story. Anthony looked as if time had stood still, and just for him. His lean body appeared well fit; his complexion was healthy, and his pretty white teeth still gleamed.

Her long lost husband sat there now, with hands folded on his knees; as he went on to tell how he and his mom had witnessed something awful his father had done. They were both in fear of him from then on. He told how his mother was concerned for their safety.

"And that's what made you leave me?" She was really hurt. "Your story is so weak. What do you want from me now?

Is this the stuff that really tests one person's love for another? She questioned.

Anthony pleaded with her to allow him to tell it all.

"No, that's not why," he was so sad.

He tried convincing her, that something had taken place right after the birth of their second child that had consequences. And that the safety of his family was more important to him, than his own life. He had been advised to disappear or his wife and children would vanish—for good.

"Rachelle," Anthony was somber. "If I had it to do again, I would. I love you and our children just that much."

His body language said it all for him. He was heavy-hearted. How could she not feel affection for her beloved, who had given up his all for his family?

Had she not just done the exact same thing; doing what was needed to protect her children?

"You could have confided in me," she was humble. "We could have faced it together. Remember our vows to each other when we met? For better or for worse, nothing would penetrate the wall of our love. It meant that two would weather any storm as one."

The estranged man had loved his family from afar. There was no other choice. However, a few close friends knew the deal and had kept him posted. He knew that his wife and children were safe, and just about everything else.

It was as if the stunned woman could feel his pain, and felt that they were on the same surgical table, two hearts bonded together—as one.

"So, are we still in harm's way," she wanted to know.

Anthony was about to breakdown and cry. He wanted to wipe away all the hurt she must have gone through without him.

"No," he carried on, "I don't think so. Something has taken place to hopefully end it all. And if it's not too late, we can be a family again. I still must remain in incognito for awhile longer."

"I'm confused," she confided, "why take the chance if it's not safe for us?"

But he could not reveal what was about to happen. He had hoped that she would trust him to make it all better. His sources were on cue and there were no mistaking the information that was passed on to him, with one exception.

"A family member passed," he went on, "and I have to handle the final arrangements,"

Rachelle was so sorry to hear of his loss. She wanted to be near him and comfort the only man she had ever loved.

"There's so much that you have missed," she replied, "by someone else's hands at threats."

The love-sick woman understood all too well, what it felt like to be in fear, to be intimidated, and made to feel helpless.

"I know that it's not going to be easy," he lowered his head, "walking back into your lives after so long. But I just could not stay away another day."

If he knew so much about the family and their everyday lives, was he also aware of her past, and the things that she had done? Starting out with doubt, Rachelle now assured herself to a point of certainty.

She would hope not. And if that were to be the case—he would never hear it from her.

"We will get through whatever happens," she asserted, "this time as a family unit. Nothing should be allowed to keep us apart—from here on."

Then she left the chair that had sustained her, while she had listened to Anthony's saga. Rachelle moved slowly toward him, as though she walked high above ground. She lovingly placed a hand on his shoulder, and took a seat beside him. Then she embraced the one and only true love of her life, hoping she might ease his sorrow.

"Sweetheart," she was very passionate, "time has balanced our being, and the choices that we have made, whether they were good or bad, voluntary or involuntary; totaled out to our pure existence."

Now, two souls who had had their share of separation were together once again.

RELEASE ME

Not long after, Rachelle called Anthony, Jr. She wanted to tell him about his father. Antionette had left for her last year of study in Italy. There would be time to tell her about the father's re-appearance.

"Anthony," trying to be calm, "could you stop on your way in. There's something we need to discuss."

There was no reason to prolong what needed to be done. Her son was an attorney, and she had hoped that being such would help him keep his cool.

"No problem Mom," he replied, "is everything OK?"

Rachelle had never really lied to her children before, and now was not the time to start.

"So far, so good," she said, "it's something that we cannot discuss over the telephone."

The plan was to speak with him alone. Anthony, Sr. thought it would be best to tread the water lightly. And she had agreed. They both did not feel that it was fair to spring too much at once on their son or daughter.

"I just wrapped up my last case for today," Anthony, Jr. responded, "I'll be there soon."

And with that, the longest three minutes she could ever remember, ended with—*love you Mom*.

Then the nervous mother, called her friends to cancel the night out with them. Of course Lori wanted to know why. Rachelle kindly said that something very important had come up, and that she and her son needed to address it. Promising to call later, she ended what could have been, relentless questions from her two buddies.

Rachelle had prepared a light meal and chilled some wine by the time her son arrived. Anthony was eager to hear what she had to discuss with him.

"So Mom," he started, "what's happening?"

He placed the fork on the side of his plate, and with both hands supporting his chin; he looked at her smiling like when he was an adolescent.

"There is no easy way to say what I'm about to tell you," she hesitated. "So here goes."

He looked at her frowning, wondering what could it be. His Mom was always cool and calm. But now she seemed a little uneasy.

"Yesterday," she tried to smile, "I had a longtime-no-see-visitor."

Rachelle paused, before continuing. She was not going to keep him guessing, but thought that she might as well take it slow, at least for a moment.

"Come on Mom," he urged, "stop with the suspense."

For a minute he reminded her of his God-mother, Lori; they were both inpatient. However, she was glad that he did not have her temper. But he was right. She needed to just let it go.

"Well," she paused, "your father is back." She was nervous.

Now what? Just waiting for him to say something was like dangling from the top of a Ferris wheel. Was it still the same day? It was like it took that long for her son to speak. Maybe, he was just letting it all sink in.

"Mom," he finally said, "I know."

Another shock! The second one within a matter of twenty-four hours; but this was way too much. The only good part about it; was that unlike the first; at least she was now seated.

"What," her voice rose, "correct me, but did I just hear you say, that you knew?"

The wise son looked concerned. He felt it might upset his mom that he knew— but had not said a word.

"I know how you must feel," he went on, "but ever since the ordeal with that Cedric guy, I've had someone tail you. It was only to assure your safety."

Now she had mixed emotions; being pissed off was first. Then he had not told her what he knew. However, she felt good knowing that her safety meant a lot to her children.

"Why didn't you tell me," she was serious. "I'm a big girl. I could've handled it, as I did just yesterday."

Anthony pushed the chair back a little from the table, crossed his arms over his chest. He looked at Rachelle, his head tilted slightly to one side.

"I immediately requested a twenty-four hour watch."

Anthony went on to say that then, he received reports that a strange man was lurking around the house. And that is when he had the person in question followed.

"Go on," she requested. "I'm listening." She was at a loss.

"So I went to the address that was given to me by the private eye." Anthony said. "I had a couple of my homeys with me just in case. Really it was only to scare the cat off."

His aim was to do more than what he had just shared with her. He had taken the snoop as someone who might do harm to Rachelle. Roughing him up was more like it.

"But as it turned out, Dad was waiting for me. While I was having him followed, he had someone doing the same to me."

This was surely a soap opera in the making. And there was much more to follow.

"After listening to Dad, I began to understand why he left," Anthony said, "I would do the same for family. There he was in the flesh, my father. I was more than glad to see him."

He hoped that the man had told his Mom everything, because it had gotten to the point where he wanted to let her know before now.

"The good thing," she replied, relieved, "is that now you know, and we can all tell Antionette together."

Another chapter of their lives had come to the fore-front, and they had settled it.

"Your father want us to attend the funeral services with him," she informed, "he said that it would be small, with only a few close friends."

"I'm ready," he said, "did he tell you what relation the deceased is to him?"

He really wanted to get to know his Dad again. He didn't feel that he was a bad person, but rather someone who would go to the end of it all for them—and that he did.

"No, he didn't say," she answered, "and I didn't think to ask. I do know that he's picking us up tomorrow morning at nine."

They finished the tasty meal, and simply enjoyed the moment.

Later they talked more about the left turn that their lives had just taken. Then they decided that a call would be made to Antionette right after the services.

It had been a long and tiring two days for Rachelle. But before bidding her son a safe goodnight, she wanted to know if he still had a watch on her. Anthony smiled, kissed his Mom. Just as he got into the car; he waved, saying: "Yes I do."

For Rachelle, time was always speeding by. She and Anthony were ready when the limo arrived. They sat in the back on one side, and his father directly across from them. It was a quiet ride to say farewell to a stranger.

"Junior, I am really sorry," the elder spoke, "that you never got the chance to meet my mother and father."

There was no reaction to what he had just mentioned to his son. But it was alright just the same. This was not the time to get into such conversations.

At the funeral home, it was just as Rachelle had been told. Only a handful of people were there to say their last goodbyes to the deceased. Nearing the casket, Rachelle lost her footing and fell to her knees.

"Mom, Rachelle," the father and son said, quickly grabbing her by the arm, "Are you OK?"

Why would she be alright? She felt that something was pulling her nearer than what she wanted. They both looked on with concern, as they walked closer to view the body.

When was it all going to end for her? There in the casket was a face she had hoped to never set eyes upon, ever again—Cedric.

"Sweetheart," Anthony Sr. suggested, "have a seat, I'll get someone to bring you some water."

The Meyers men stood looking down on the body of the father, having done so much wrong, that he and his mother had; to flee from their home in the middle of the night, to be free of him.

Anthony Jr. viewed the man lying there; having no idea that he, who had stalked, terrified, kidnapped, and raped his Mom, was actually his grandfather.

Soon after that horrifying ordeal, the family began to mend their broken ties. It would take time to heal their bruised hearts, but they would work at it.

Anthony Sr. moved in with his wife, and things were beginning to look up. His father had left everything to him and his family.

Somehow, Cedric had found out that Rachelle's son and daughter were his grandchildren. He had known that Rachelle was his daughter-in-law. But because of his lust to have her, that fact was pushed aside.

Although, Cedric was a thug and a bully, his businesses were legit. His wife, after leaving him, changed her name from Elderry to Meyers. It solved the question as to why Anthony's name was different from that of his father.

While Anthony was busy running things, including hiring and firing, Rachelle had focused on other projects. Lori and Lisa were aware of almost everything that had taken place.

Then Rachelle took sick after a week or two, writing the illness off as a cold or perhaps overworking. Maybe it was the excitement of knowing; that her daughter was taking a leave from classes to come home— at last meeting the father she had never known.

This was the family that Rachelle and Anthony had always dreamed of having. They planned one big gala, with family, the children, Aunt Vera, Uncle Gilbert, and her main buddies and their spouses.

Everything was catered, and an events coordinator was hired, taking away the stress of Rachelle having to do it all.

Needless to say, they were all happy. Aunt Vera and Uncle Gilbert finally hooked up, Lisa and Jerome were now married, and Lori was expecting her first child.

Soon it was time for Antionette to return to class, and she wanted her family to spend a few weeks in Italy with her. It was not a good time for her brother who was working on a top notch case, and her father had taken on another restaurant. However, her Mom could make the trip, but to stay for only a week.

Before leaving, Rachelle made an appointment to see her physician. She wanted to be cleared for the trip, and to maybe get a prescription for some antibiotics.

"Well, Mrs. Myers," her doctor reported, "everything looks just fine except the one test that confirms you are about six weeks pregnant."

Now was the time to really pass out. What the hell! Anthony back in her life, and after less than two months—this! She was sure that the term, turning red was out the window, because for sure, she just knew that all the colors in the rainbow had visited her face.

"Oh no Doc," she panicked, "there must be a mistake, do the test again."

There was no need; he had run more than one already.

"I'm really sorry Mrs. Myers," he tried to calm his patient. I took another after the first one. But there's more."

Dear Lord, what is going on? More does not sound good at all. She waited, heading for an anxiety attack. The mother-to-be was certainly on edge. Her vocal cords had taken a hike, and left her to face the music.

"You are having twins," the doctor went on, "but everything will be just fine. I will keep a watchful eye on you and the babies. You know, you are still a young woman."

What was she going to do? It was bad enough, that she was with child, but then, to be thrown a fast ball, two babies. Life had it in for her.

She was knocking at the *door of old age*, and when it opened, forty-two would be starring directly in her face.

"But doctor I can't be pregnant," she was short of breathe, "I had my tubes tied twenty years ago. This is not happening to me."

First, she would find that SOB who performed the procedure, and kill him dead, then she would sue the hell out of the hospital for hiring the fool.

"Mrs. Myers," he tried explaining, "a few cases have been reported, where the tubal ligation did not work. That is, after awhile, the tubes came loose."

Now you tell me. What good was it going to do, hearing it now?

The damage was done. She would go on her trip, and deal with it when she returned home.

One day, she might just write a book about the many times life had kicked her buttocks. Why not turn it up; for one last round. Rachelle had circled the globe—of misfortunes, now she was in full orbit.

⁂

Italy was all that she had pictured, and more. The food was delicious, the wines were superb, and the scenery was breathtaking.

Antionette was doing great with her classes and adapting well to her new environment.

Their time together was serene. Her daughter had made friends with a few classmates, and was very excited for them to meet her Mom. Rachelle was amused to find that some of the things that were said about Italian men were true.

She observed them as being really passionate and romantic. The couples appeared to be so much into one another. Many of them held hands, when strolling together in the square; while others embraced, sitting along the waterfalls. It was just so beautiful.

It broke her heart having to leave her baby girl in a foreign country all alone, so far from home. Assuring her Mom that she would be home for good, before long, made Rachelle feel a little better.

When Rachelle returned home, the word of her pregnancy was great news for everyone, but still she questioned it. It was not because she wanted to end it. It just was not planned. She had thrown in the towel for motherhood awhile ago. Hell, it had been so long, she might not know how to be a new parent.

Sure Anthony was walking on clouds. Now he would have a chance to be a daddy again. It would be akin to starting over. Soon his children would be too busy with their own families to spend quality time with him and Rachelle.

He had given out many cigars, and bottles of wine, that might have been used to make a down payment on another business. But that was a man thing. Rachelle looked at those gestures as gifts in a man's baby shower.

Then why should the women have all the fun? It was senior's way of celebrating the new baby.

At least, she was spared morning sickness. And that was good because she was able to go with Antionette, and have a wonderful time in a foreign country.

At home again, then back to the drawing board; Rachelle was burning her candle at both ends—so was Mr. Meyers.

Rachelle had to deal with Lori and Lisa's bickering about who would be the child's godmother.

"Well, I know one thing," Lori boasted, "I can teach my god child more things than you."

She had started again with Lisa. But it was about time to shut Lori up.

"Say what you may," Lisa said, "you had your chance with Anthony Jr., now it's my turn. So, suck it up, and let it go, smart ass."

I bet, I told her. Lisa admitted to herself, leaving Lori standing in the middle of the floor, with her mouth wide open. The startled female was not use to Lisa being sharp with her.

THIS IS IT

Rachelle's tired eyes watered, but she watched closely anyway. Her loving attention does not waiver. A most precious soul places a wicker basket—full of various medications—on a folding table, very close at hand. It is not an easy scene; both parties suffer. The sick man draws serious concern; he is really blessed to even be alive. While his vigilant wife looks over the man's life-threatening illness. Rachelle is more like a doting mother eagle guarding a fallen fledgling's recovery.

With considerable difficulty, Anthony chooses one pill bottle after the other; he is still dazed from the last round of meds. So he is careful to pick each container; reading the many different labels, with drug names that he cannot understand. Common remedy, such as basic *aspirin*, would be welcome to the ailing spouse. But these prescribed drugs have either Latin or "laboratory listings."

Nevertheless, Anthony was mindful to handle the medications carefully to avoid dropping them; because with that happening, there was always the possibility of crossing dosages. *Dangerous!* Rachelle, the loyal wife knew that her poor husband could hardly afford the risk of ingesting a wrong drug combination. The dutiful woman continued to take note, ensuring he did the right thing.

It broke Rachelle's heart as she continued to watch her husband eyeing that big basket of doctor-recommended drugs stationed at his left side—the surviving half—as the right had been stricken and severely limited by bilateral strokes. Of course, Anthony's suffering was founded by serious conditions like internal bleeding and pneumonia. The bright side was that he was alive at all.

The assortment of meds is pigeon-holed in seven columns (one for each day of the week) of plastic square wells; and each line consists of four tiny compartments: labeled MORN/NOON/EVE/BED. It seems that medicine taking, is maybe a 24/7 proposition with him. His pitiful condition requires a certain regimen. It consists of pills and capsules…or else. While remaining to be a twice-a-day necessity he adheres to…or something else.

Rachelle's empathetic heart goes out to him. At times she questions herself as to what she would do in a similar situation. But his is not a condition that one (of sound mind) would likely trade place with.

In Anthony's disposition, no one would senselessly volunteer to be in his troubled shoes. Strokes and a massive cardiac arrest are no small ailments to deal with. Yet he survives a succession of debilitating blows to somehow eventually rise as a "walking miracle." Surely God most definitely had been a merciful Father to an extraordinary recipient of a grand-great blessing.

Yes, there are limitations now in a list of things that some folks take for granted: to eat/shave/bathe/prepare meals and so forth. Rachelle wipes the tears away with nearby facial tissues. She understands that a sudden loss of independence strikes a resounding blow to her beloved man's ego.

As a former and primarily right-handed person, his commitment is to "only try" and accomplish things with the same dexterity of an infrequently used left-hand. It is as awkward maintaining a balance that is oftentimes accompanied by dizziness and otherwise light-headedness.

Then there are many times when Rachelle desperately wants to do everything for Anthony, but is reluctant, she does not want him to feel helpless. She observes that despite these demanding daily trials, he seems remarkably strong and resilient. He appears determined to overcome the setbacks. Her tried spouse has much to offer, still.

Then tears over-whelm Rachelle as the painful visions of the incident haunt her memory. The telephone call on a rainy night, that caused her heart to stop momentarily. And the voice on the other end informing her that Anthony had been forced off the highway over a deep embankment. And that he was being air lifted to a Med-Star Hospital for emergency care.

With nerves like jumping jacks, and mass confusion thoughts; she quickly called her daughter to drive her to the given location. But on the dark, wet, and foggy highway; unfamiliar about the quickest way to get there and how; there they were, being lead by the Hand of God.

Upon arrival, and meeting with the surgeon, needless to say, expectations for Anthony's survival were rather dim. The doctors and other surgical staff held little hope for him.

Then Rachelle found herself kneeling in the chapel near the family waiting room. There she prayed to God not to take him from her. With hands folded close to her heart, and poor vision from salty tears, she pleaded to the only one who gives blessings, who takes and gives life, to spare Anthony's.

A little later, standing and shaking uncontrollably, she took a seat. With her face in hands, Rachelle continued to pray to the Heavenly Father.

Because she knew deep within; that no matter what was taking place on that surgical table, God and His Angels had the complete authority. And in a whisper, she heard, "everything is going to be OK."

Rachelle shuddered at the thought of paramedics having to shock Anthony four times, before getting a heartbeat. Literally, he was not breathing for as long as 34 minutes.

Once again; she wiped her watery eyes with one of the many, dainty handkerchiefs that Mom had given her sometime ago.

When asked if he remembers what happened to him, Anthony would sadly look away for a moment, then responded with a crisp, "no."

Then with a stroke affected smile, he says he only recalls certain people looking down at him—in the ICU—telling him that it was going to be alright.

He thought he was dreaming. As for Rachelle, she remained a total wreck! But in an odd way, his wife was glad that he did not remember that horrifying time.

Several motorists who witnessed the accident reported that the car behind Anthony's appeared to deliberately run into the back of his vehicle; forcing it over a deep embankment.

It was said that four men were in a dark blue pick-up truck that sped off right afterward. An all point bulletin (APB) was issued in hopes of apprehending the automobile and its passengers.

Subsequently, an anonymous hit had been ordered for Cedric's life. Whoever caused it wanted the foul play to look like a highway accident.

It was really painful for Rachelle to think about. Anthony had been mistaken for his father. And ironically, it all took place after Cedric's death.

Surely, there was a definite line between life and death—and Anthony held onto it by a very thin thread. And with the prayers of many—and God's grace—Anthony pulled through slowly. Yes, it was true that *when praises go up, blessings come down.*

Rachelle believed that she had never seen a miracle; but surely witnessed one during her husband's ordeal.

The right side of Anthony's body was now limited. Speech was slurred. Movement was awkward—with paralysis that renders little or no feeling at all. Yet and again, his left side functions as it did prior to the series of dangerous health issues.

His handwriting style continues to be child-like and nearly illegible; however, with each attempt it gets noticeably better. Then mentally, he was fairly sharp; but at times may question something, that he may have forgotten. There are days when there was a recurring element of doubt with him; but that was OK.

There were many nights, when she would watch him closely to ensure that he was breathing in his sleep. And other times when he would leave home, she remained on edge—until he called to say he was on his way.

Retrospectively, the medical team could not provide a reasonable explanation as to how Anthony, was a surviving "miracle" patient. But there was no question in Rachelle's mind over whomever or whatever had made it all possible.

Rachelle was still the designated protector of her family and friends. Then in her heart, she strongly believed that her husband was kept here on earth, giving him a second chance to be there for his family—including new twin sons.

The pitcher of life was not through with the batter—Rachelle. During the delivery of Durrian and Dermum, there was a problem. Something was not right.

Durrian, needed a procedure, to address a serious problem. Blood had to be drawn and tested, along with DNA samples. The results sent Rachelle into a whirlwind.

Her sons had separate fathers. Durrian was Cedric's and Dermum was Anthony's. Only she and the doctor knew, and he was bond by confidentiality to his patient.

How could she confess to her husband, that in death, his father still managed to haunt them from the grave?

Sometimes, things more or less took place for a specific reason. But why was it that the past finds a way to upset things, so many have worked diligently to level off?

One could never go back to multiply choices of the past. Yet and still, yesterday had somehow brought them here. Then tomorrow was surely out of reach. But, today was where Rachelle and Anthony would begin anew.

Made in the USA
Middletown, DE
25 September 2016